D1553279

The
Night
I Freed
John
Brown

Patricia Lee Gauch, Editor

PHILOMEL BOOKS
A division of Penguin Young Readers Group.
Published by The Penguin Group.
Penguin Group (USA) Inc., 375 Hudson Street, New York, NY 10014, U.S.A.
Penguin Group (Canada), 90 Eglinton Avenue East, Suite 700, Toronto, Ontario
M4P 2Y3, Canada (a division of Pearson Penguin Canada Inc.).
Penguin Books Ltd, 80 Strand, London WC2R 0RL, England.
Penguin Ireland, 25 St. Stephen's Green, Dublin 2, Ireland (a division of Penguin Books Ltd).
Penguin Group (Australia), 250 Camberwell Road, Camberwell, Victoria 3124, Australia
(a division of Pearson Australia Group Pty Ltd).
Penguin Books India Pvt Ltd, 11 Community Centre, Panchsheel Park, New Delhi -
110 017, India.
Penguin Group (NZ), 67 Apollo Drive, Rosedale, North Shore 0632,
New Zealand (a division of Pearson New Zealand Ltd).
Penguin Books (South Africa) (Pty) Ltd, 24 Sturdee Avenue, Rosebank, Johannesburg
2196, South Africa.
Penguin Books Ltd, Registered Offices: 80 Strand, London WC2R 0RL, England.

Published simultaneously in Canada.
Printed in the United States of America.
Design by Semadar Megged.

Library of Congress Cataloging-in-Publication Data
Cummings, John Michael.
The night I freed John Brown / John Michael Cummings.   p. cm.
Summary: In Harpers Ferry, West Virginia, thirteen-year-old Josh uncovers family
secrets involving his overly strict father, whose anger threatens to tear the family apart.
[1. Family problems—Fiction. 2. Fathers and sons—Fiction. 3. Harpers Ferry
(W. Va.)—Fiction.] I. Title.   PZ7.C912Ni 2008   [Fic]—dc22   2007023648
ISBN 978-0-399-25054-5
10 9 8 7 6 5 4 3 2 1

The Night I Freed John Brown

Dear Michele,

Enjoy the adventure!

Cordially,
John M. C

P.S. Thanks so much for inviting me to your class!

JOHN MICHAEL CUMMINGS

PHILOMEL BOOKS

To Susan, whose faith in me and devotion to my work have forged the friendship and love of a lifetime

Also to my mother, for her unfailing kind support over the years

Acknowledgments

Jessica Regel, my agent, for her steadfast encouragement, exceptional narrative instincts, and professional commitment.

Patti Gauch, my editor, whose eminent talent and hands-on work have shaped this novel and made it flourish.

I would also like to acknowledge Kiffin Steurer and Tamra Tuller for their invaluable editorial contribution resulting in many fine improvements.

Finally, there have been other skilled readers of this story, in some form, at one time or another. All have contributed, with my gratitude.

Additional Acknowledgment

An excerpt of this novel was previously published as the short story "Cowmint" in *Sandstone Review*, Issue 5.

Chapter 1: GO AWAY, GHOST!

MY NEW FRIEND LUKE hopped the rusted chain hanging low and heavy across the overgrown lane and caught up with me where the weeds became thick and dead trees lay everywhere. We had just entered a secret junglelike world. Vines curled down like snakes, and dark trees stood around like villains and thieves. Blanketing the ground were purple wildflowers and gooey webs of silver leaves. Dead ahead were the ghostly white ruins of a chapel, its jagged walls biting up through the black earth like bad teeth. Nearby, in speckles of sunlight, stood a vine-wrapped statue of the Virgin Mary, her arms missing. You could almost see her waving hello to us.

From here we crossed a meadow high with dandelions, then stepped through skinny, ragged trees that stood like scarecrows below a tall white house on the hill. Luke was looking up and stumbling. Though the house had been empty for years, it was still snow-white and gleaming, as if just painted.

"Wow, it *does* look just like my house!" he said, running ahead, his voice husky and excited. "You weren't kidding."

You bet I wasn't kidding. Luke was my new next-door neighbor in town. A month ago, he, his father, and two brothers moved into a house that was a spitting image of this one.

He stepped closer. It was creepy how impossible it was to tell the houses apart, and he knew it. There was no other word for it. *Creepy.* Here, in these woods full of broken-up dormitories and armless statues, stood this perfect copy of his house in town, sealed in time for some reason.

"Wait, was it just painted?" he asked, turning around.

"No, it always looks that way," I said, grinning.

He did a double take.

"No way," he said.

As if alive, the house stood tall and shimmering bright-white. My mother said it was like the tall evergreens beyond it—everlasting. I thought it looked like cake icing.

When I stepped up onto the porch, Luke took a step back.

"You sure nobody lives here?" he said. "'Cause there are blinds on the windows."

More than that, in one of the windows, a single venetian blind was lifted up, making a sliverlike black eye peeking out at us! Luke came off the ground like a scared cat.

"Jesus, there's somebody in there!"

"No, there's not," I said, laughing.

I had already explained it all to him. This was the old caretaker's house for the Catholic retreat, the ruins of which we had just walked through. My grandparents had once been the caretakers, and my father had grown up in this house, working the dairy farm by the river.

But Luke was convinced someone was still living here. Backing up more, he pointed to a broom leaning against the house, and a welcome mat in place. Grinning and shaking my head, I swung the front door open for him to see—inside was an empty kitchen, with bare, dull-white walls and an outline where the refrigerator and sink had been removed long ago.

"See?" I said.

Luke inched his way inside behind me.

"What's that?" he hissed, pointing his skinny arm so hard it looked like a knobby branch.

On the musty counter where the sink had been removed, leaving a gaping hole in the wall, sat a brand-new salt shaker with a shiny metal top and bright-white salt inside. I stopped and looked at it, puzzled.

"See," he said, turning to leave.

"Come on," I said, grabbing his arm.

Down a dark hall we went, the narrow ceiling looming over us like a long spaceship.

"And it's just unlocked?" he whispered, looking up.

"Yeah, the church left it this way."

When we came to stairs with fancy banisters, we stopped dead. Luke turned in a complete circle, and I turned with him, slowly, as if we were tiny figures in a music box, the strange house turning around us, without the music. Overhead was a maze of stairs, where, in the rows of handrails curving up and around, were hundreds of hiding spots for eyes.

"*Weird*," he said, breathing the word out.

No cracks in the plaster, no missing handrails, no broken glass, everything just sitting and waiting.

"Josh, this is *exactly* like our house!"

The sharp hiss of his voice set loose a thousand spiders up the dim walls around us, their scampering little legs rattling like dried leaves.

"Told you," I said.

I stood following the walls with my eyes, seeing the distance each door was from the next, where the windows were cut in, and how it all folded together. It reminded me of art class. It was as if somebody had traced Luke's house in town and stuck the copy out here in the woods along the river to keep from getting caught at cheating.

Luke bent down and ran his hand over the floor, then sat crouched, looking at his clean palm.

"It's like somebody just moved out," he said. " . . . does anybody else know about this place?"

"Just my family."

"Just your family?"

I took a step toward the banister.

"Wait," he said, popping up. "What happened?"

"I'm not supposed to talk about it, okay?"

I stood there for a moment, my hand on the smooth railing. Anybody could hear it in my voice—I was dying to talk about it.

" . . . there were some things stolen out of here," I said, starting up the stairs.

"What things?"

He was so close I could feel his warm breath on my back through my shirt.

"Church things," I said.

I made a little show of sitting down on the stairs. Luke was quick to sit on the step below me.

It happened many years ago, when I was around seven. The chapel, the dorms, this house—all were picked clean. Silver statues. A gold leaf altar filled with ivory figures. Even candles. Everything taken.

"'Robbed blind, goddammit!'" I cried out, in a hushed roar of my father's voice that scared away all the devil eyes in the stairs above us.

Doors were found busted open, I told Luke. Windows broken. Supposedly the railroad police were called in, as the tracks near here were also damaged.

"They even took fingerprints and everything," I said, leaning back against the wall.

Luke sat riveted on me, his eyes angled up with the handrail.

"Was anybody caught?" he asked.

I shook my head. Everybody was sure suspected, from the neighbors upriver to the neighbors downriver. Even the Brothers were accused at one point.

"After that, the church just totally forgot about this place."

What was left fell into decay. The barn, the pump house, the orchard—all gone.

"Except this house," I said, looking up again at the countless eyes peering down. "It's like it's alive."

We sat for a moment longer, looking up into the deep stairs. Then I pulled myself up by the handrail.

"Come on," I said.

Up and around we went, past empty room after empty room, our whispery voices scampering ahead, filling the house with spiders. In the second-floor hallway, sunlight was angling in, elongating our shadows into twenty-foot monster men, the dark doorways on either side like jail cells we were being led to.

"It's like a clone! Only unfinished," Luke said.

It was true. Where in his house in town were bright rooms full of antiques and things that made a home, here in this house along the river were empty rooms, squares of space, with one door and one window in each. Nothing else.

Without warning, Luke cried out, pointing and backing up, "What the hell's that!"

Dancing on the ceiling were a dozen soft spots of light, as if from weak flashlights moving in a jerky circle.

"Reflections off the river," I said, laughing. "Look." I pointed to the bright window down the hall.

His nerves shot, Luke shouted at the top of his lungs—
"Hello!"

"*Hel-lo!*" the house shouted back.

We cringed as if plaster and beams were coming down. Luke burst out laughing at my terrified face.

"Josh," he said, a moment later, "this place is really weird. It should just be used for something."

"Tell me about it," I said, walking ahead of him.

"No, I mean it. Somebody should live here again."

He caught up with me and looked over, his eyes shining through his wire-frame glasses.

"Wait, why doesn't your family live here?"

"'Cause it's not for sale. That's why. The church owns it."

He stopped. I stopped. He stood looking at me. I wasn't lying. The church did own it, and they would never sell it. For years, the railroad had tried to buy it. So had big, rich families in town.

Still, I knew what Luke was thinking. Why was I showing him this house as if my family already owned it? Why had I just taken him back into these woods, making this old, empty house into a big question mark I wanted him to solve?

Drifting away from me, he poked his head into another room.

"Man, it must bother your father like crazy. I mean, he used to live here."

It killed him, was how Mom always put it.

"And he *never* comes back here?"

"Not since my grandparents died," I said.

"Never?"

"Never," I said.

Luke turned and looked at me. His glasses, whenever he scrunched up his nose, slid up and down like a toy.

"Is that why he's so mean?" he asked.

Spiders on the walls stood still, listening for my answer. Outside, in the weeds, the armless statue suddenly frowned, and the trees around her slouched, and the wildflowers drooped. The great mysterious feeling of being in this house—the gleam in my eyes, the thump in my chest—funneled down and disappeared into one small word: *mean*. For eighth graders like Luke and me, it was just the right-size word. Whoever you were, you were either mean or you weren't.

I looked down at the floor.

"Guess so," I said.

Luke, shaking his head, peered into another room. The same—just empty.

"But why's the church not using it for something?" he asked.

I was taking the stairs ahead of him, getting ahead of my own tour.

"I don't know, okay?" I said.

We soon stood on the fourth floor.

"Hey, my room," Luke said in a hushed voice, peering into the room that, in his identical house in town, was his room.

It was like a before-and-after photo. In this room, there were nothing but bare, sad walls and a lonely little window. In Luke's room in town stood a big bed with four posts that rose up toward the ceiling like giant screws.

"Hey," said Luke, looking all around as he walked through this shadow room, "does Ricky know about this house?"

I felt an ache in the pit of my stomach. Ricky was Ricky Hardaway, my no-account cousin. He did odd jobs around town, including some painting in Luke's house, which was how Luke knew him. Most of the time, Ricky was in jail for drugs. He was nobody I wanted Luke to think I was related to, or even talk about.

"Nah," I said, looking away and leaving it at that.

On the fifth floor, the top floor, we came to the room facing the river. This had been my father's bedroom when he was a boy. Now it was like every other—totally empty.

"Whoa, whose is that?" Luke asked, pointing at the grungy mattress that lay in the corner.

It was small, like a boy's mattress, long ago stripped of its sheet, with prison-gray stripes running down it and branded crossways by lines of rust from the bedspring that once held it.

"Some bum's," I said.

He looked over at me. "Bum? You've seen him?"

I nodded, lying about it before I knew it.

"You mean, you come here by yourself?"

"Sometimes," I said.

"Your brothers?"

I walked over and kicked the mattress.

"Sometimes."

He stepped up beside me and kicked it, too.

"Both of them?"

He didn't have to ask about both. If one did, the other did.

I never saw Jerry or Robbie out here, but I knew they came. I could see it in their eyes at home—that look of having wandered through a cemetery all day.

Luke stepped past me and up to the window, where he looked down at the overgrown field. He saw a herd of slow-moving, vine-covered elephants, rhinos, and zebras, inside of which were a tractor, a wagon, a plow, a few old cars, and even a flatbed truck—junked farm vehicles that, over the years, the underbrush had crawled right over, weaving a topiary garden out of. I saw a grassy pasture filled with cows, and my father and Uncle Dave shooting clay pigeons out over the river. Mom and Grandma were on the porch below, sipping lemonade and watching the speedboats zoom on the river, leaving white waves in the water as they pulled in and out of the landing on the far side.

"Hey, I wonder if you can see my house," Luke said, squinting through the dusty glass, then shielding the sun with his hand to try to see downriver toward town.

When I said nothing, he glanced back at me.

"Can you?" he asked.

I shrugged and acted nonchalant about it, but I had wondered. I knew you could see the church steeple in town, way in the distance, as a glitter of gold in the sky. On clear days, you could also see the red roof of the armory. So you ought to be able to see Luke's house, too, since it was so tall, like this one. But for some reason, you couldn't.

"Bet I can," he said, peering out the window again.

I watched him squint as far as he could into the distance. It was strange watching him do something I had done before.

Luke was from Boston. He was thirteen like me. He was short and skinny like me. But he was nothing like me on the inside. He didn't have a mother to baby him, because his father was divorced. He wasn't shy. He spoke right up to adults and didn't hang his head. He acted as if he could go anywhere, do anything. He knew Paris, he knew London. He had even been on that bullet train in Japan that went 175 mph! But as different as he was from me, this house talked to us the same, made us wonder and think the same.

I stepped up to the window beside him, and together we looked as hard as we could toward town. In this direction, I could stare forever, trying to figure out why I lived down there, why this house was here, and why my life was going back and forth between these two places.

After a moment, Luke held his arm up to the window.

"Hey, look," he said.

In the light I could see goose bumps on his forearm.

"You were serious, weren't you?" he said, his voice quavering.

I looked at him.

"About what?"

"About this house being alive."

I stood frozen.

"'Cause I have news for you," he said, his eyes going wider and wider.

"What?" I said, grinning and leaning away from him.

"It's waking up!" he shouted at the top of his lungs.

He bolted from the window, hopped the mattress, and dashed out the door, only to hit the brakes and come back. As I stood grinning, he reached in, grabbed the doorknob, and slammed the door shut behind him. *Bang!* The sound clapped up around me, freezing me. For a second, I just stood there. I was alone in my father's childhood bedroom, sealed in. Around me walls rose up and drew across the ceiling into a perfect cube, trapping me inside, like a mosquito inside a gob of sap.

Running from the shiver of it, I sailed over the mattress, flung open the door, and took off after Luke. Down the long hallway we ran, screaming one long scream, pretending we were falling out of an airplane. We took the stairs in a flurry of feet, pushing and bumping each other, me on Luke's heels, him on mine. In our mad dash down the hallway to get to the next flight, the dark doorways on both sides moved and blurred like coffins filled with mummies and zombies that were stepping out after us.

"Go! Go! Go!" Luke was shouting, waving his arm like a marine sergeant.

Down and around, down and around, and down and around we raced. Coming after us, along with the mummies and zombies, were the thousands upon thousands of spiders, an army of creepy-crawlies now scampering down the long, high walls, just seconds behind us.

We galloped halfway down one flight, then leaped— falling through the air down to the landing, our sneaks thumping down one-two. One banister, I hopped and rode down like a slide, knocking into Luke and sending both of us headlong onto the landing below. Laughing, trampling over each other, we scrambled on.

On a floor near the bottom, Luke stopped to slam a door. *Boom!*

"Go away, ghost!" he barked, pointing his finger at the closed door.

He dashed to the next door and did the same. *Boom!* "Go away, ghost!"

I joined in on the other side of the hall. *Boom!* "Go away, ghost!"

Down the long hall we went, slamming doors, barking orders at ghosts. But some of the doors bounced back open, and the mummies and zombies spilled out of their coffins again.

"They're waking up!" Luke yelled. "They're waking up!"

We shrieked and howled, marking up the walls of this copycat cheater house with our big mouths. By the time we got to the bottom, Luke had twisted his ankle and was hopping on one leg. But he wasn't hurt bad.

Off the shaded porch and into the sunlight we charged, yelling like soldiers. We ran down over the hill, then stumbled through the scarecrow trees and out into the high meadow, laughing our guts out, then falling and lying on the ground to catch our breath.

Behind him the big white house rose up tall.

"Look at the windows!" I cried out, pointing.

There must have been twenty, all black and shiny.

"Look how they're all looking at us!" I cried.

They *were* looking at us.

Out of the corner of my eye I saw Luke look over at me. He didn't have to say it. I already knew. We had gotten away this time. Maybe next time we wouldn't.

Chapter II: FROM JEFFERSON'S ROCK

WHEN WE GOT BACK to town, we still had time before we had to be home, so we scrambled up the long path to Jefferson's Rock, slipping on loose stones, tripping over roots, then giant-stepping over boulders. At the top, we hauled ourselves out onto the sun-baked ledge by hooking our fingers into the deep grooves of initials carved in by Civil War soldiers long ago.

"Charles M. Parnell," one read. "Prv. 8th MO INF. 1861. 'Died For Love of Country.'" Over these carvings were the soft-stone chicken scratches by tourists—"I love Sandy L." and "Terry Mitchell, Dallas, TX." The whole pancake-shaped rock, marked up with names and initials from left to right, top to bottom, was like a yearbook of the Civil War. Or a gravestone.

Once scooting out into the center where it was safe, Luke and I sat up cross-legged and looked out at the famous view. This was historic Harpers Ferry, West Virginia—home of John Brown's Raid! On a dark night in 1859, the abolitionist

John Brown and his band of raiders came charging into the town on horseback, shooting up the place, trying to capture the town's armory for guns to fight the war against slavery. Half of them were killed, and Brown was captured and later hanged after a big trial. Today, tourists came here from all over to gawk at the old brick firehouse where they stabbed Brown with a sword—you could barely make it out below, a tiny square of faded red between two darker buildings.

Everything from our school history book to old paintings to souvenir T-shirts showed this view. You could see the St. Peter's bell tower standing straight and tall over the town, like Abe Lincoln's hat. The famous Stone Steps—a hundred crooked steps carved out of solid rock!—zigzagged down between old buildings. On the grassy knoll to our left, the white gravestones in St. Peter's Cemetery tilted against each other like dominoes.

After a few minutes, I talked Luke into standing up on the rock with me. We did, but stayed crouched at the knees, as if surfboarding over the town. Blue sky wrapped around our heads while sunlight blazed down. You could even see the curve of the earth from up here! Luke and I had the whole summer ahead of us—June, July, and August—and the months were as big as the pale-green mountains around us, climbing into the clouds.

I pointed to trees that grew limbs only on one side, because of wind constantly blowing them in one direction. Around them were birds riding the wind currents up from the riverbank.

"Blur your eyes," I told Luke.

"What?"

"Blur your eyes. See the wishbone?" I said, pointing. "The big peace sign?"

Below, two rivers, one green and fast, the other brown and slow, came together in the shape of a giant wishbone. Railroad bridges lay across them, hinged together at the train tunnel on the far side. A big waterfall poured down in the middle of the fast green river.

Luke, his eyes crossed, was grinning and nodding.

"That's Maryland over there," I said, pointing to the left. "And Virginia over there." I pointed to the right.

I didn't have to tell him we were standing on West Virginia. I also didn't have to tell him you could stand in all three states at once, on the neck of rocky land below.

We looked all around for a while, even far off to the left to try to see my grandmother's old house back up the river, though that view was completely blocked by trees now. Then I reached out, pretended to grab half of the great wishbone, and yanked.

"What'd you do that for?" he asked, looking over.

"For a wish. That I can go to art school in the city someday."

He gave me a blank look. Luke was from the city. There were probably ten art schools around his old house in Boston.

We sat on the big rock, leaned back, and tried to gaze a hundred miles into the gap in the mountains to see the missilelike Washington Monument. Luke was soon bored with this, and I understood why when he told me he had been up in the Eiffel Tower in Paris. He started pointing down at rooftops of town—bright red and blue squares flickering below us like puzzle pieces flung through the trees.

"Hey, look," he said, pointing at the glistening green roof right below us, "my house!"

Luke sat staring down at it, saying he was seeing doubles. Then, as if he couldn't help himself, he pointed at the only rusted-up little roof on the street—my house, right beside his.

"Look, your house," he said, grinning.

I was instantly knotted up inside, seeing how small and poor my house looked beside his. The big rust stain on our roof was hideous. It looked like God had spit Red Man on our home.

"Wow, it's like the church is gonna fall right on your house!" Luke said, grinning even more.

He was right. To the left of our house was Luke's big house. To the right of us, St. Peter's Catholic Church. Our house was crouched down in the middle, as if trying to hide under the trees, while the big church steeple stood ready to squash it like a giant's foot.

"Whatta you all do there?" he asked, looking over at me, his nose wrinkled up.

What did we *do* there in the house? We lived there! What did he think we did there? It was the strangest question, the most horrible question. Still, I knew what he meant. Why was my family living in a national park in the first place? My father didn't work for the park, like his father. We were just living on the historic hill, letting our house fall down, while the rest of the houses were being restored by the park. Sooner or later, everybody wondered why Bill Connors and his family lived on the hill.

"Dad had a shop once," I said.

Luke looked at me.

"In your all's house?"

I nodded. *Yes,* in our crappy little house!

"What kind?"

I shrugged.

"Souvenir shop. Sold candy apples and Civil War stuff."

"Did he like it?"

I thought for a second. If I nodded, I'd only have to answer more questions, tougher questions. If I shook my head, I'd only feel worse for having a father who couldn't even like having a shop that sold candy apples.

"I don't know," I finally said.

Out of the corner of my eye, as I saw Luke still looking down at my house, I cringed inside knowing he was getting an awful eyeful—the weeds and trees in our yard Dad let grow high to try to hide our embarrassing little house from the gawking tourists on the front street; the old boards and junk he had stacked up; and, worst of all, the pig paths my brothers and I had worn through the trees, trying to find a secret way to leave our house without being seen by tourists. There must have been a dozen sneaky little zigzagging paths through the trees around our house you could see from up here on Jefferson's Rock. Funny, Dad had built up all this crazy hermit camouflage in our yard, but all the thousands and thousands of tourists had to do to laugh at our house anyway was just hike up this trail, sit out on this rock, and peer down from above. Up here our house was like a man with all this shaggy hair in front, but an embarrassing bald spot in back.

After a moment, Luke looked over at me.

"And he really doesn't allow you all to have friends over?" he asked.

I laughed a horrible laugh inside. *What friends?* Even if we had any, we sure wouldn't want them seeing our ugly house up close: the dirty plastic covering the windows, the white extension cord holding up the rain gutter, and the gnarly firewood heaped up on the sagging back porch. To say nothing of the inside of the house: the rotted plaster-board behind the toilet and the hole in the kitchen ceiling over the water heater.

Yes, my father had this horrible little rule. *No one allowed in the house. Keep the doors closed. Don't attract attention.* He had other horrible rules, too. *No going into shops. No going into museums. Stay clear of the rivers, tourists, and park rangers.*

Out of the corner of my eye, I saw Luke still looking over at me. So I jumped up tall on the rock again, my sneaks squashing the initials of Civil War soldiers, and roared out in my father's voice, "'I don't have a front yard! I don't have a backyard! I don't have a driveway to myself! I can't go outside without a hundred damn tourists looking at me!'"

I glanced down to see Luke smiling.

"'But a man's home,'" I went on, swaggering around on the hallowed rock, "'is a man's home!'"

With Luke laughing, I stopped yelling and looked out. Here I was on the highest spot around, as close to heaven as I could be, standing where Thomas Jefferson more than two hundred years ago wrote the famous passage, "A scene worth a voyage across the Atlantic," where Stonewall Jackson had carved in his initials, too, where everyone famous had come—but all I could see suddenly were the dark cliffs across the river frowning down at me for making fun of my father.

Or at least I thought it was because of me. There was another reason the cliffs could be frowning.

"My brothers!" I suddenly cried out to Luke, pointing down at them coming up the trail toward us.

Without a sound, we slithered off the back of the rock, crouched, and watched.

Jerry and Robbie sure stood out among the colorfully dressed tourists on the trail, especially Jerry. He had that *I'm-getting-big-and-belligerent* West Virginia look, wearing a flannel shirt with the sleeves rolled up and cruddy old jeans that really showed his bowlegged walk.

Seeing my brothers out in the town was like looking in the mirror at the worst time. We were not clean-cut, cute boys like the tourist kids, or like Luke and his brothers for that matter. Jerry had a small, red, scrunched-up face that looked to be in pain all the time. Robbie had a chipped front tooth; old Sharky, they called him at school. And thanks to Dad giving us crew cuts every month with a Sears home barber kit, we looked like cue balls.

Crouched down behind Jefferson's Rock, I felt almost

sorry for my brothers as a crowd of tourist girls came walking toward them on the trail below. They were pretty, blond, and wearing private school uniforms. You could tell they were rich and had everything in the world from the way they were giggling. Robbie looked sweaty and miserable as they passed. Jerry had his head down, as if he had something embarrassing on his face and was daring anybody to tell him about it. Then my brothers nearly knocked into a fat tourist woman by the guardrail, and she looked over at her husband in disgust.

Luke, leaning over to me, whispered, "Did they really shoot out Lee Jackson's window?"

Jerry wasn't nicknamed "The Mad Sniper of Harpers Ferry" for nothing. One time he started shooting at tourists from our rooftop with his BB gun, and they went running down the street, crying out, "Bees! Bees!" Police and park rangers came to our door and took away my brother's BB gun. They made him sit in the back of a squad car for an hour while Dad talked them out of pressing charges, which, apparently, they could have done, even though my stupid brother was only fifteen at the time. Now he was sixteen and twice as bad. On top of that, he had another BB gun. Robbie was no better.

Luke and I, before my brothers could spot us, scampered down the sandy trail behind Jefferson's Rock to the cliffs in the hillside below, where the ground was bare and sparkled with the tops of beer cans.

"In here!" I hissed, hurrying Luke into a cave behind me.

"Did they see us?" he asked, looking back.

"I don't think so."

I stood lookout at the cave's entrance until sure my brothers had gone on up the trail, probably to throw rocks down on the road below, scaring cars. Then Luke and I crept back into the cave, peering up at big faces of ugly rock leering down at us. The air inside was cool and moldy-smelling. Water was dripping all around, and the ground was nothing but loose stones and mud, with daylight disappearing behind us.

"Wow, this place would be perfect for John Brown," he said. He spun around. "Hey, he probably hid slave children in here!"

We started looking around, hoping to find something John Brown had left behind—a musket, a message on the wall, shackles and chains he had broken off slaves.

Luke, as it turned out, knew everything about John Brown from his father, who was a historian for the park. Luke had even read John Brown's diary, which told of him riding seventy miles at night on the underground railway, taking a wagon from Michigan to Virginia, then back to Kansas, in the dead of winter, with a price on his head! According to Luke, along the way, Brown delivered a baby, wrote a book of poetry, and, in Abilene, Kansas, stood in as a preacher for a Mormon congregation.

"No way!" I said, hearing all this.

"Well, the guy was a visionary," he said, winging a rock across the cave, which thudded against the far side.

My father would keel over if he heard this. John Brown was not a good name in my house. First of all, we lived across the street from the John Brown Wax Museum, where there was a big wax figure of John Brown in one of the windows, glaring at our house day and night, creeping us out. On top of that, our front steps were always littered with little red John Brown Ice Cream cups from the John Brown House down the hill, which Mom was constantly picking up. We had John Brown's Fort, John Brown's Farm, even John Brown's Cave. We had a bridge, highway, and tunnel named after him, too. There was even a big annual town play about him. Dad said if one more thing was named after him, he'd put a brick through the picture window across the street.

Luke stopped to peer up at the ceiling.

"It just made him angry that he couldn't get enough volunteers to fight slavery," he said.

I looked down at my untied shoestrings. My father got angry for no reason.

Suddenly, roaring like a crazy man, Luke charged across the cave and hopped up on a big rock in the corner.

"His sons died for him!" he said, thrusting his arms overhead. "*Yeah!*"

"They *died* for him?" I said, peering over at him. I never heard that before.

He nodded, all proud of this fact.

"All of them?" I asked.

Luke didn't know for sure. Oliver and Owen Brown did for sure, he said, at the fort in town. Two others, he thought, were killed in other battles.

As we rolled the big rock across the cave floor like a steamroller, crunching smaller stones to bits, I couldn't help but think that my brothers would probably give our father a heart attack someday, rather than die for him.

Then Luke stood peering up at the ceiling of the cave again.

"Hey, which is it," he said, "stalactite or stalagmite that hangs down?"

I wasn't sure. The words were so close I couldn't even guess. Luke thought the stalactite hung down, since that word seemed to be said more than the other word and that kind was less impressive than the kind that grew up out of the ground, which there were none of in this cave. It was funny thinking, but I knew just what he meant.

We started jumping up and down, trying to grab one of these rock swords hanging down.

"Was he religious?" I asked.

"Brown? I think so."

"But he was mean," I said.

Luke stopped jumping and looked over at me.

"Yeah, but only to people who deserved it."

"My father's just mean," I said, sitting down on the very rock we had rolled to tie my shoelaces.

Shoes tied, I found a stick on the floor of the cave and starting doodling in the dirt. Luke stood watching. The cave was quiet around us except for the scratching sound of my stick echoing up the sides.

"I can't believe your father likes my father," I said, looking up at Luke.

"Dad gets along with everybody," he said with a shrug.

That sure must be it, because my father got along with

nobody! After the two ladies who had lived in Luke's house died a few years back, Dad said there wasn't anybody around worth getting along with or being neighborly to.

Living in a tourist town, we didn't have regular neighbors anyway. There was that gay antique dealer two houses up Dad never waved to. So Jerry threw rocks on the man's roof. There was that couple in the red house behind ours Dad didn't like because they were Seventh-day Adventists. So Jerry poured kerosene in their flower garden. The rest were snooty park types or gawking tourists.

I looked up at Luke.

"What's he like?" I asked. "My father at your house?"

"Oh, he and Dad just talk about stuff," he said, shrugging.

About stuff? What stuff? Nuts-and-bolts stuff? Definitely not John Brown stuff. No one in my family could figure it out. Dad started going over about a month ago, and he just kept going. Late in the afternoon. After supper. On weekends. But I never went over to Luke's house while my father was there. He'd only yell at me or say something horrible to embarrass me.

I went on doodling in the dirt.

"Would you, you know, die for your dad?" I asked Luke.

"Yeah, sure," he said. Then he grinned at me. "Would you?"

It was a horrible thought, with an even more horrible answer. No, I definitely would not die for my father, and not just because I hated him, but because he wouldn't want me to. I wasn't good enough to die for him.

He had nothing to admire about me. I didn't have a

strong back or an "interest in tools" like my brother Robbie. And I didn't have stamina like my oldest brother Jerry. I had been a sick kid, and now all I did was draw "kooky art," as my father called it, give him back talk, then run to Mom. She said it was an unwinnable situation for both of us.

Sitting on this rock in the cave, I looked up at Luke again and said something I couldn't stop myself from saying.

"You're lucky you get along with your father."

But it was like I had flooded the cave with lights, ruining the moment. Luke stood still for a moment. Then he turned away.

"What?" I said, my voice echoing back into the cave.

What?

What?

What?

But he wouldn't even look at me. He wouldn't even say anything. He actually took a few steps away.

"Well, you are lucky," I said again.

I didn't get it. His father had a good job with the park. Mr. Richmond acted in plays at the Old Opera House in Charles Town. He had "flamboyance," as my mother called it. He was happy all the time. Luke *was* lucky. So what was so wrong with saying so?

"Seriously," I said.

Finally, Luke turned to me.

"Damn, Josh," he said, his voice hard and cold, "why do you keep feeling sorry for yourself?"

I froze. I couldn't believe he just said this. His words shot down from the cave's ceiling like stalactites or stalagmites, whichever they were, and they shot up from the cave's floor like them, too.

I stood helpless as Luke turned and started out of the cave without me. Left alone, I looked up at the stupid rock spears hanging down. I even threw a beer can up at one, trying to bust it off.

A moment later, I stepped out of the cave, into sunlight and warmth, and caught up with Luke down the trail. Neither of us said anything until we reached the railroad tracks and started walking side by side, kicking the wine bottles and tin cans that lay between the rails.

"You all coming over Saturday?" he asked.

I could hear dread in his voice. Renovations to his house were finally done, and my entire family was invited over Saturday evening to see them.

"I don't know," I answered.

In my heart I was just as worried as he was. As many times as I had already been over to Luke's house, I had never been over there with my parents and brothers before, and Dad made us all crazy. Jerry turned into a worse bully around him. Robbie had a mean streak, too, that Dad brought out. Mom, who hadn't been inside Luke's house yet, was totally jealous of it already, having had to live this past month beside a house getting fixed up right in her face. I didn't want to be seen with any of them.

Luke and I walked on toward town, not saying much. Bolted to the creosote-stained timbers of the train bridge ahead was a rusted-up yellow sign that read, DO NOT GO BEYOND THIS POINT. But this sign wasn't for me. No, I'd go all right. I wasn't my father, and I had my own separate life, which just then included going right up the front steps of the Richmonds' house with my crazy family on Saturday.

Chapter III: To the Richmonds'

S ATURDAY EVENING, JUST TWO days later, Dad, Mom, and I got dressed up to go next door to the Richmonds'. At the last minute, Jerry and Robbie managed to get out of going by claiming they were sick, which really meant they didn't want to be embarrassed by something Dad would say in front of everyone. Dad was happy not to have them along, saying they'd only cause trouble. I actually tried to get out of going, too, but Mom said only two of us, at the most, could be sick at the same time. Then, looking for a decent belt to wear, Dad yanked another cracked-up strap of leather out of his closet, tossed it aside, and said, "Katie, I'm having second thoughts."

So was I. Second thoughts. Third thoughts. It would be a miserable night for sure. I was standing beside Mom over by the ironing board, waiting for her to finish ironing my favorite blue shirt. She stopped gliding the iron up and down my sleeves and looked over at my father.

"Second thoughts? Why on earth, Bill?"

"Because that damn man attracts too much attention over there," he growled. "That's why."

"Niles Richmond?"

Mom glanced at me, then stood waiting for Dad to explain.

"The other day," he said, rooting through his closet, swatting around the pant legs hanging down, "he had that damn Father 'Ron' over there."

Mom set the steam iron down on the end of the ironing board. Standing up straight, it hissed like a shiny rocket about to blast off.

"In Perky's old house?" she asked, her face dented with worry.

Dad popped his head out of the closet.

"No, not 'Perky's' house, Katie. *Richmond's* house now! And, yes, over there."

They stood staring at each other, a million words being said between them in silence.

Just as John Brown was not a good name in our house, neither was Father Ron. As far as my father was concerned, Father Ron was the one who had ruined St. Peter's Church next door. He put an end to catechism classes and opened a church garden for tourists instead, along with some silly play school for park families. He made other changes as well, including allowing tourists to wear shorts and tank tops to mass. He was one of those liberal priests who went by his first name. Father "Ron," Dad said, twisting his mouth up as if tasting a bad persimmon.

Mom snatched up the iron and went back to rubbing its shiny triangle nose across my shirt.

"Well, I'm sure Niles Richmond is just being neighborly, Bill," she said. "There's sure nothing wrong with a little of that around here."

"Too damn neighborly, if you ask me," he muttered, his head again buried in clothes hanging down in the closet. "He knows everybody in town already. Lee Jackson—Richmond had him next door, too."

Wearing my troublemaking grin, I chimed in, "Mr. Richmond has Ricky working for him, too."

Dad, popping his head out of the closet again, zeroed his eyes in on me until his face looked chiseled out of red rock.

"He's nobody to smile about, buster," he said.

"No, he's not, Josh," Mom was quick to say. "Poor boy's got a rough life ahead of him. You should feel sorry for him."

"No, hell, don't feel sorry for him. Just stay the hell away from him, you hear? All of you all." Dad raised his head to the ceiling. "Jerry, Robbie, stay the hell away from that Ricky Hardaway over there, you hear!"

As he went on hunting through his closet, swatting his own pants and shirts around, I laughed inside at the thought of him slapping and beating himself up for a change, instead of one of us.

"Damn dope-smoking SOB," he went on muttering. "Probably steal something next door first chance he gets. Mark my words."

Mom stopped swishing the iron and held it raised over

my shirt. It hissed and gagged as her tight grip strangled it like a serpent.

"Bill, please," she said.

"And that busybody woman who works for the park," Dad went on, "drives that little red sports car, Katie—he had her next door, too." He popped his head out of the closet again. "Before you know it, I'll have half of Harpers Ferry trooping over next door."

"Well, you already do," Mom said, sliding the iron up and down my sleeves.

Dad stood leering at her.

"What the hell's that supposed to mean?"

She pointed her free hand at the thickest wall in our house—three feet of Shenandoah Valley limestone. Dad always said the best thing about living in a two-hundred-year-old armory worker's house was having three-foot-thick walls so that he didn't have to hear the damn church bells next door. Or the tourists down in the street. Or any other noise for that matter.

He glared at both Mom and me, then only me, until I could feel his eyes burn through me. It was a burn that went back as far as I could remember.

"Pick up your pencils, buster," he growled now, pointing around the room.

Finding another belt, he wrapped the ends of it around his hands and gave it a good snap.

"Josh," Mom whispered, touching me on the shoulder, "pick them up—hurry."

I hurried around the room, picking up my Prismacolor pencils, snatching up red and blue ones wherever I found them, white ones off the arm of the sofa, green ones off the TV table, collecting them all as fast as I could.

"Fifty cents a damn pencil," he muttered. "Must be twenty, thirty dollars lying around on my floor."

"Well, Bill, he needs that brand."

"*Needs that brand?* Why?"

"Because they're—"

Mom turned to me.

"Oil-based," I said.

"Oil-based, my foot," he said. "Buster, pick them up."

As I stood with a fistful of pencils, watching him go on trying to find one decent belt to wear, muttering to himself the whole time, I knew what was really eating him. He was just nervous and ashamed about tonight. I felt the same way every day of my life getting ready for school, and especially getting dressed up for the yearbook picture. There was nothing like a big event to make you feel poor and ugly inside.

As he went on to gripe about his dull razor, then about someone having used his comb, I saw his eyes stopping on every ugly spot in our house—the dry rot around the bathtub, the buckle Jerry and Robbie had put in the plasterboard in the hall, fighting, and the downstairs steps worn bare of paint. Dad couldn't stop feeling sorry for himself. Just like me when I was around Luke.

Finally, after all the ironing, fussing in the mirror, and Dad's complaining, we were ready to leave.

"The front door, Bill?" Mom asked, standing in the middle of the living room, her big orange purse draped over her arm.

"Well, we can't very well go through the trees tonight, can we?" he snapped.

In my family, we never used our front door, on account of all the tourists always down on the sidewalk, ready to gawk at us. Even in the evening they were there, due to the John Brown House now being open until eleven in the summer. But tonight, we had to use the front door because Mom couldn't make it through the trees in her low-heeled shoes.

"Now don't go turning on the damn porch light, Katie," Dad muttered. "No need attracting more attention than necessary—come on."

The three of us slipped outside, onto the front porch. The evening light was nearly gone on our side of the trees that covered our house like a tent. Left was a spotty, dim, greenish air that made it seem we were living inside a pair of army fatigues. To Dad's annoyance, Mom stopped to straighten the welcome mat so that it covered the big crack in our step.

"Oh, hell, Katie, do you have to do that now?" he griped.

He hurried us down the steps. At the bottom, a big maple limb hung down, like a curtain for us to step through. Waiting for us on the other side was the tourist-filled world of Harpers Ferry—souvenir shops, park rangers on horseback, and tourists in every nook and cranny on the street. This evening, we stepped through the curtain to find half a dozen soda cups waiting for us on our bottom step. *Pop!* My big foot landed right in the middle of one, exploding Coke all over my sneaker. Half the street turned as if I had shot a gun at them.

"Dammit it, Josh," Dad growled. "I told you not to attract attention."

"Well, Bill, it's not his fault," Mom said.

She stooped in her good J. C. Penney skirt to pick up the leaky cup. Then, aggravating him all over again, she started back up the steps with all the leaky cups in her fingers, dripping them on our good concrete. He stood muttering at the bottom of the steps, glancing in both directions at the tourists heading toward us. He became antsier by the second, as if we had just robbed our own house and were taking too long to get away.

"I don't know why the hell she has to bother," he grumbled.

In moments like these, I wondered whether he wanted me to respond. It seemed he was asking me a question, as if he thought I were older suddenly, as if we were alone in the world and he wanted me to be his friend.

"Because she wants a nice house, Bill," I wanted to say, as my mother's friend who knew how to answer for her. "She doesn't mind living under the trees. She just wants a nice house, Bill."

Finally, Mom came back down through the big limb, but then stopped to reach over into the flower bed and straighten up the Private Residence sign that kept falling over. Dad stood there with his hands on his hips.

"I suppose you'd like to sweep the porch while you're at it?" he said.

"Well, it could use it, yes," she said.

He popped out a laugh that said she was the hardest woman in the world to deal with.

We started up the sidewalk. This was historic High Street—gaslit, cobblestone-covered, and lined with wrought-iron fences and restored blue and gray clapboard houses, most used as souvenir shops. Tourists dressed up for the Thomas Jefferson Inn up the street and the Frederick Douglass House down the street were getting a good look at us as we passed—Dad in his worn-out factory-gray pants he thought was "dressing up" because Mom had ironed them, Mom with her big orange purse from 1980, and me with a huge blotch of embarrassment on my face for all of us.

"Look at 'em gawking," he muttered.

As I walked behind my father, my insides felt as bowed out as the wooden slats in the old-time flour barrels that lined the street as decorations. I watched as he kept his head down. Catholics always hung their heads low when they needed to repent. And Dad needed to repent. He was our ringleader. He was the one who made our yard cluttered, who left our house tattered, our car faded.

Finally, we were at the Richmonds' front door. Mom was all eyes, and though I had been over here plenty of times before, being with her, it all seemed new to me, too. The big porch curved around the house like the back of a piano, and the many white posts under the long handrail looked like a hundred overflowing vases of milk. The shaggy lawn had been cut as close as a golf course. Orange and yellow flowers burst from big clay pots. Fat baby angels made of granite stood on either side of the tall white columns—Dad grumbled that he was surprised my brothers or me hadn't broken off the fingers by now. On the top step, Mom was so silly about not wanting to put her shoes on the brand-new American Eagle welcome mat that Dad all but pushed her up to the door. He knocked, then opened the glistening green door, and the three of us entered together.

Chapter IV: HOUSE OF MIRRORS

NSIDE WAS A PALACE of sparkling chandeliers, curvy vases taller than me, and window drapes that fell like waterfalls of blue and gold. Walls and ceilings were decorated like cakes, with curlicues in the wallpaper. Furniture sprawled along the white walls like new cars in a showroom. All around were fancy old things made of copper and bronze.

I turned to see my mother's gaping face.

"See, I told you," I said, grinning along with her.

I strolled in ahead of both her and Dad and onto a thick purple rug. Every time I came into this room, I stopped and stood smiling at myself in the many mirrors, imagining myself a king. Mirrors in gold frames. Mirrors in silver ones. Mirrors reflecting mirrors. So many large and small that each seemed to be looking at another, and so on, bouncing reflections half a dozen times over.

Seconds later, Mr. Richmond appeared under the high ceiling down the hall, his shoes clicking across the glassy marble floor. Dad immediately went into his "personality routine"—what my brothers and I called it when the park rangers came to our door and Dad didn't know whether Jerry and Robbie had shot out more windows, so he had to be all smiles and jokes until he figured out whether he could just go back to being as ornery as ever.

Mr. Richmond had his own personality routine. He said his hellos, and my mother was full of smiles. For a moment, it was dizzying—my parents talking and laughing, being normal people, Mr. Richmond all but putting his arms around them, the whole house glittering around them like Christmas presents under a tree.

"Where's Jerry and Robbie?" Mr. Richmond asked, peering around behind my parents.

"Oh, hell, Niles," said my father, "you don't want them over here. They'd just break something."

Mom turned to him with a frown.

"Goodness, Bill, don't say that."

"Well, Katie, you know it's true." He turned to Mr. Richmond. "You can't trust a kid anymore than you can a damn dog." Then, he put on a big grin to try to be charming. "Unless you put a millstone around his neck."

Mr. Richmond stood with a smile that said he wasn't sure what he had just heard.

For my mother and me, this was our first chance to see Mr. Richmond and Dad together up close. I was pretty sure why Mr. Richmond was "interesting" to my father, but why Mr. Richmond could stand my father for an instant—that was a complete mystery. They were as different as chicory and crabgrass, as my father himself would say. Mr. Richmond had on a shirt my father wouldn't use as an oil rag, it was so colorful. But more than that, they seemed to speak different languages. Dad was all cusswords and short sentences, and Mr. Richmond said everything with a comma at the end, as if he never planned on finishing. Still, they got along for some reason.

Mom, looking around, said she *absolutely, absolutely* did not recognize the place. She pointed to a Georgian-style walnut mirror that she said should be hanging in the governor's mansion. In no time, she and Mr. Richmond were talking antiques—Ridgewood chifforobe, Blakely love seat, Neapolitan paintings.

I felt so bad for my mother. As much as she knew about antiques, all she had in our house was a broken spinning wheel and a broken push-pedal sewing machine to put her Lemon Pledge on.

When she asked Mr. Richmond how in the world he had come by all his beautiful antiques, he said, in a manner that made her blush, "Effort, generosity, and . . . luck, Katherine."

Suddenly, my father laughed out loud.

"Effort, luck, hell. You mean *money*!"

I was wondering how long he could hold his tongue. Two minutes tops.

Mr. Richmond, meanwhile, didn't seem to hear my father's little remark. He just went on showing us around. In one room were big-framed pictures of Mr. Richmond's sons, Daniel, Alex, and Luke, who, Mr. Richmond said, were at the store and should be back shortly. In the pictures, Daniel was standing in front of the St. Sebastian Cathedral in Le Monde, France; Alex, the Leaning Tower of Pisa, which even I recognized; and Luke, the ruins of the Roman Coliseum. Mom's face was one big smile. She had never seen more adorable boys, she said—and so fortunate, to have traveled at a young age.

The Richmonds had luck all right.

"Is their mother . . . ?" she asked.

"Wilmington, Delaware," Mr. Richmond said, suddenly becoming all tightlipped.

But I already knew he was divorced, so he didn't have to hide it from me. Mom neither. She was raised Methodist. Dad was the one he should be worried about. Even I knew from just my one year of catechism that Catholics didn't allow divorce—although in Father Ron's church, who knew?

"Oh, that reminds me," Mr. Richmond said, stopping. "We're putting on a little read-through of *Othello*. Would your sons care to participate?"

Mom stood stock-still, her face hollow-looking.

"Read-through?"

"Oh, nothing big. Right here in the house. Just my sons and me. We love Shakespeare. We could use a few extras," Mr. Richmond said, smiling.

Mom turned to Dad.

"Bill?"

"Well, don't ask me, Katie," he said, probably freaked out

by just the thought of stage lights on my brothers and me. "They're your damn kids."

Mr. Richmond, getting no clear answer, smiled and left it at that.

"As long as it's not about 'you know who,'" Dad went on to mutter.

I was pretty sure Dad didn't know *Othello* from a marshmallow, but I couldn't be sure whether Mr. Richmond knew that "you know who" was John Brown.

In another room was a huge old painting of George Washington like the one I saw on my school trip to Washington. Around the rest of the room were marble-top dressers—three in this room alone. And books. There must have been a hundred, all with shiny dark spines. Books so old and fancy Dad said my brothers and I were not to touch them even though Mr. Richmond said we could.

All Mom could say at this point was that she was impressed, very impressed.

"Well, I've had good help arranging it all," Mr. Richmond said with a smile.

"Oh, Niles, don't say that," said my father. He looked over at Mom. "Katie, he means that damn Ricky."

"Well, he's perfectly reliable," he said, looking puzzled by all our reactions.

Dad was frowning. Mom was shaking her head in disbelief. And I stood grinning at Mr. Richmond. For a good reason, too. As nice and smart as he was, he sure didn't know Ricky Hardaway the way we did.

. . .

THE FOUR OF US STARTED up stairs with red velvet carpeting on each step and more mirrors on the walls, one of which Mom identified as an Amish twig mirror.

"Tell her why so many damn mirrors, Niles," said my father.

Mr. Richmond was quick to do just that. "I always encourage my sons, Katherine, to see themselves from every angle."

Dad stopped and looked back at Mom. "Isn't that the damnedest thing you ever heard?"

My mother had more tact. She knew when not to say anything.

At the top of the stairs was a huge street map of Washington, DC, dated 1779. The small streets came out from the center like spokes on a wheel. Down the hall was a tall American flag standing straight up like a guard, and beside it on a stand was Abraham Lincoln's head made out of iron. Nearby was a chair Mom absolutely loved. It had pink designs and looked old and new at the same time.

"My lord, Niles, it's stunning," she said, looking around.

"Yes, stunning," my father sighed.

"Bill?"

"Well, I'm just agreeing, Katie."

She shook her head at him.

As we went up another floor, Mr. Richmond turned to my mother and said, "I understand from Luke that you all have a white Victorian like this one in the family?"

A rock fell through my stomach. It just kept falling, like in a bottomless pit. Both my parents came to a stop. Dad looked like a box of blueberries had just been smeared on his face.

"Yes, similar to this one," Mom said, standing still.

"No, *just* like this one," I said from the step below them.

My big mouth surprised me. It surprised Mr. Richmond, too. He turned and looked at me, his eyes wide and full.

"*Just* like this one, Josh? You know, that's what Luke said, too."

I nodded and grinned.

"No, hell, not 'just like,'" growled my father, all but elbowing me. "Don't listen to him, Niles. He's imagining things."

Old killjoy was quick to spout off that this house and the one I was blabbing to the world about didn't look alike at all, and even if they did, it was only because they were ordinary "Low Victorians," which were all over the county, so there was no reason to make an issue of it. I swear that man was a blind liar.

I looked up at Mr. Richmond, ready to complain to him as if to a teacher. They were too the same, and they were special because of it. No other houses around town looked like them. They went straight up, like milk cartons, and had more windows on each side than you could count, almost like a kid's drawing.

"It's like a castle," I told him, trying to get the last word in with Dad.

My father pointed his big finger at me. "Katie, hush him up!"

This was my true father. How could Mr. Richmond ever stand him long enough to talk about nuts and bolts—or whatever they talked about?

"Ask Luke!" I said to Mr. Richmond. Then I turned, gave my father an ugly face, and blared out—"You just wish you had this house!"

There. I had said it. The truth clapped out of me in a blinding white flash. In my mind it lit up all twenty of those dark, lonely rooms up the river in my grandma's house, and in the same instant it filled all twenty rooms here—going up and around, and down and around, in and out, using Mr. Richmond's mirrors, whatever it could. Then, like thunder and lightning, the moment was over.

Mr. Richmond stood looking at me, surprised I had shouted. This was the other side of me—mouthy, hating my father, full of backtalk grown-ups didn't understand. But Dad sure knew what I meant. This house was bright, happy, and full of nice furniture, just what he didn't know how to have in our house, or in any other. Just what Grandma didn't know how to have either, which was why under all the magical white shingles on her house were the darkest, barest rooms.

Mr. Richmond put on his pleasant face, as if none of this were happening. Dad, letting his shoulders fall, put on his slippery grin.

"Niles," he said, changing his tone, laughing a kooky laugh, as if what he was about to say was too silly to say, "my damn boys, especially this one here, are under the notion, thanks to their mother here—"

"Now, Bill—"

"—thanks to their mother *here,* that I should have gone to work for the park or something. Be easy on them all the time. Have a big house like this one."

Yes, that was exactly what we were under the notion of, but the way he said it, he made us all seem like idiots. Looking at Mr. Richmond and seeing his face, I was starting to figure out how he got along with my father. He could put up with Dad's temper. But not his lying.

"Just two ordinary Low Victorians, Bill?" he said.

"Yes, that's what I'm saying—Low Victorians. They're all over the county. Niles, you know that."

When Mr. Richmond just stood smiling at him, saying nothing, Dad was forced to turn to my mother for help. But she was no help. That left him ready to yank down the chandelier.

"Why in the hell am I the only one making any sense here!" he exploded. "The only damn reason that this house *might, might* look like my mother's old place is the damn gypsum in the shingles."

"Gypsum?" said Mr. Richmond.

"Yes, gypsum, Niles—and don't stand there, smiling. You know about gypsum. It's why this damn goofy kid of mine thinks that this house, or that one along the river, or both—I can't figure out his crazy head—is made out of 'cake icing,' or some such damn foolishness."

I wished the chandelier would fall on him. I wasn't a damn kid, and I wasn't foolish. And I knew that, if you wanted to get technical about it, the "gypsum" in the shingles was what made the paint last so long. It was an old building material no one used anymore. But gypsum or not, that didn't make Grandma's any less wonderful to look at.

Mom, meanwhile, had stepped away from all of us and now stood over by a window, looking down. I was happy to move over beside her. Below was our rust-stained roof, all the more ugly-looking in the dirty-orange streetlights. Casting a big Dracula shadow over it was the gigantic steeple of St. Peter's that, even at night, looked ready to topple over on our little house, across the whole vacant lot between us.

"Isn't this the window where Perky used to sit, Bill?" she said. She turned to Mr. Richmond with a smile. "You'd be interested in this, Niles." She looked back at my father. "Bill, the cowmint story?"

He waved her off with a scowl.

"The cowmint story?" asked Mr. Richmond.

Dad's little aw-shucks act didn't work on him. Mr. Richmond insisted until my father came over to the window. Mom and Mr. Richmond gathered around, but I stood back. It was a stupid story with a stupid ending, one I had heard a million times before.

AS THE STORY WENT, when my brothers and I were really young, our backyard and Perky Murphy's yard grew together, in one sloping meadow of weeds, with no fences or trees separating them. No one thought about which side was whose. We were all good neighbors then. The town was still filled with natives, and my father, if you can believe it, was actually known as a kidder. Bill the kidder, they called him.

He joked and teased until he had our neighbors frustrated and laughing at the same time.

For some special reason, the patch of ground between the two houses was full of rare plants with strange names—lamb's quarter, buttonweed, dog fennel.

"You never saw such damn variety in your life!" Dad told Mr. Richmond, tapping on the window as he pointed through the darkness at the lot below.

He knew all the plants by sight, too, as he had a hobby of studying field guides. Buckthorn. Quack grass. Pigweed. It was the damnedest thing, he said, that they all grew here together, when according to his field guides, half of them shouldn't be a thousand miles of one another. It had to be special soil, or the weather in the valley.

At this time, Perky Murphy and her older sister Mae were still living. Both were in their eighties and in wheelchairs often at this window, or on the porch below us, looking down at the town. Whenever they saw my father coming along, swishing his shoe through their weeds, looking for whatever special plant he could find next, they leaned forward to get a good look. One evening, with my brothers and me tagging along, my father stopped and stared down.

"Mae, dammit, lookie here," he said. "You know you have cowmint growing?" Only once he had marked the spot did he glance up at the old woman. "Dammit, girl, you need to get down here and get this cowmint up and into a planter."

Old Mae let out a cackle. "Billy Connors, you stop that and come up here."

Mae knew weeds well enough to know there was no such

thing as cowmint. There was horsemint. It had pink flowers. There were spearmint and peppermint of course. Everybody had heard of them. There was even something called penny mint, with purple and white flowers. But no cowmint.

"Lookie here, June, more," Dad said.

Perky's name was not June. Dad teased her that way because her sister was Mae, like the month of May. "You know how valuable this is?" he said, looking up.

Perky, unlike her sister, knew nothing about weeds. She was so bad she thought Queen Anne's lace was embroidery. Looking down at my father, she was bug-eyed. She glanced over at her sister, who was keeping a straight face.

Mr. Richmond, as he listened to my father the storyteller, was not keeping a straight face, however. He was grinning and nodding and shaking his head.

"So," Dad went on, "I yelled up at her—'June, damn your heart, there must be a million bucks' worth of cowmint just lying around down here, going bad! You want your neighbors to get it all?' Well, you know what she did, Niles?"

Dad stood there with a big grin, keeping Mr. Richmond in suspense. Mom was grinning, too, enjoying this part of the story the most.

"Well, not two minutes later, that damn woman—she must have been eighty-five, right, Katie? Hadn't taken a step on her own in twenty years—well, she came a-high-stepping down her back lot . . ." Dad lifted his knees high and threw up his arms, like a puppet flopping around on its strings. ". . . shears in hand, pail in the other, ready to collect her fortune!"

Dad bent over at the waist and wheezed out his pipe smoker's laugh. Mom was holding her hand over her mouth as she shook with laughter. Mr. Richmond was grinning hard, ready to laugh, wanting to laugh, but was more curious of my parents and this unbelievable story.

"So she could walk?" he asked, looking first at Dad, then Mom. "Or couldn't?"

"She could indeed, after that," answered my father.

Mr. Richmond's eyes went wide.

"Even though you just made up that plant?" he asked.

Dad stood there with a grin and devil ears, the same look my brother Jerry always got into trouble for.

"I just put two words together, yes," he said.

Mr. Richmond glanced left, then right, then shifted his weight and crossed his arms.

"*Just put two words together?* Bill, did you ever tell her?" he asked, glancing back and forth at my parents.

"Never did," Dad said, turning and looking back out the window at the famous patch of ground below, now overgrown with trees or covered with junk or thinned out to bare rock. Staring down into the darkness, he looked almost sad for a moment. "Old June, or Perky, went to her grave believing there was such a thing as cowmint—and right in her backyard."

Mom took a step away from the window, closer to Mr. Richmond.

"And she was a lot happier for it, too, Niles," she wasn't afraid to say. "She lived another, what, six, seven years, Bill, and never used that wheelchair again."

"Never," said my father, shaking his head. "She ended up walking all over town." He pointed in the direction of the lower town, a smile breaking over his face. "Why, I saw her once over on the Stone Steps—and there's a hundred of them to walk up!"

I couldn't take my eyes off Mr. Richmond, he looked so stunned. A strange light bathed his face. His eyes were as shiny as marbles. His mouth was falling open.

"So what about the plant, Bill?" he asked. "What about the plant?"

Dad looked at him as if he had never been asked this question before.

"Oh, as far as I know, Perky forgot all about it," he said.

"Forgot all about it? Forgot all about it!"

Looking at Mr. Richmond, I had never seen anyone so impressed by my father.

"That's a most remarkable story, Bill," he said. "You cured that woman!"

Cured? I turned to Mom, grinning. She couldn't believe what she was hearing either. Dad, I didn't recognize. He stood there suddenly like an important man who had just done something that should be remembered, talked about, put in a book, chiseled into a stone, something.

Mr. Richmond turned to my mother and me.

"See where a little imagination can get you?" he said.

He had a gleam in his eyes and a square set to his jaw that reminded me of Luke talking about John Brown, jumping up and down in the cave, calling him a "visionary." I couldn't believe it—Mr. Richmond was acting like my father was one of the famous men who had made history in Harpers Ferry!

"Oh, Niles, now don't go twisting the situation," Dad said, trying to sound annoyed. "Katie, say something?"

My mother did say something, but not what Dad wanted.

"Well, Bill," she said, with a song in her voice, "it worked on Perky. You saw it with your own eyes."

Mr. Richmond looked at me.

"Josh, you believe cowmint exists, too, don't you?" he said. "Just like your father?"

I nodded—I nodded because I liked Mr. Richmond, but also because I liked how he made my father seem.

He stood pointing his finger at me as if I'd won a big prize.

"And you'll be another famous Harpers Ferrian for it!" he said.

In that second, I saw myself becoming another Thomas Jefferson or Abe Lincoln standing on Jefferson's Rock, thinking famous thoughts to put in a book someday. I wasn't living in my crappy little house and hiding from tourists until I couldn't stand it anymore, only to sneak out to Grandma's empty house. I was somebody, like Luke.

Dad, meanwhile, turned to Mom, his hands on his hips.

"Katie, would you put a stop to this nonsense, please."

But Mom was grinning. Mr. Richmond was grinning. I was grinning. Poor Dad was outnumbered. We were all happy, even if he wasn't, or wouldn't admit it.

．．．

THAT NIGHT, THE MOONLIGHT was so bright, glazing the blue walls around my top bunk, that I drew in my sketchpad by it. Using my best Grumbacher 2B pencils, I let my imagination fly. I drew flowers with wings, flowers with eyes, flowers with shooting flames.

Mr. Richmond was the greatest. You bet I believed in cowmint! As I worked, I dreamed I was a great artist in history, like Francisco Goya. We had studied him in school this year. He knew how to make fun of the world and make great paintings of it at the same time. I didn't want to make fun of the world. I just wanted to be happy in it.

Soon I was drawing more than flowers, anything and everything I could think of—an eggbeater for some reason, then the outline of the state of New Jersey in flames. My hand moved as if under a spell, sometimes ripping the paper with the point of the pencil. Jerry and Robbie were snoring below, but my top bunk felt like a magic carpet above the world.

I leaned over the bunk and looked out the window, trying to see the lights of the Richmonds' house, but the dark trees in our yard blocked them. When my eyes instead drifted across the street, I saw, for about the billionth time in my life, the wax figure of John Brown in the big picture window in the museum, aiming his rifle at our house.

All my life I had been looking down John Brown's barrel. When I was little, Mom said my nightmares were because of him. In my scariest dreams, John Brown came to life, crashed through the picture window, shattering it all over the street, and started toward my house, the long bayonet gleaming on the end of his rifle. For the longest time, I believed he was angry with everyone in my family because of all our yelling he had to listen to.

Tonight, though, I wasn't so scared of John Brown. Holding my drawing pencil like a pistol, I fired back at him—"BLAM! POW! RAT-A-TAT!" I grinned at how free and silly I felt, thanks to Mr. Richmond.

Quietly, I climbed down the bunk bed ladder, found my brother's binoculars in his dresser drawer, and crept back up. Sitting cross-legged on my bed, I looked through the binoculars, aiming them across the street and turning the focus knob until the blurry, lighted picture window came in clear and John Brown's angry face jumped into my eyes point blank. Magnified ten times, his mean, snarling face filled my eyes from corner to corner! His eyes were bloodshot. His beard was as coarse as rusted barbed wire. His fanglike teeth bit the air like a Neanderthal's.

As I stared him down, I wondered if hotshot Luke would like John Brown so much if he had to grow up in this house, had to sleep in this bed, with a father yelling downstairs and a wax madman glaring through this window upstairs, never knowing why either man was so angry.

But tonight I didn't wonder for long. Tonight I didn't care. I let the binoculars drop on the bed and went back to drawing flowers.

CHAPTER V: ON THE COWMINT TRAIL

THE NEXT MORNING, I WAS up bright and early, for the first time ever, looking for cowmint in the vacant lot. I didn't think for a minute that it was some miracle plant, but I was determined to find it anyway. I didn't have to have a reason why. I waded right into the high weeds and started pawing around, the prickly leaves and hard stems stinging my bare legs. When I saw Mr. Richmond walking past our house in his forest-green park uniform, heading to work, he called out with a wave, "Ask your father. He knows what it looks like."

I knew what mint smelled like and, from Dad's field guides, could see what all the mint plants looked like. Horsemint, which I figured was closest to how cowmint would look, had a purple flower sticking straight up.

Moments later, Mom called across the yard to tell me that if I was going to traipse around in the weeds, I *must, must* wear long pants and a long-sleeved shirt.

"I don't wanna have to take you to the doctor with poison ivy," she said as I came into the house to change.

Watch out for snakes, too, she said. Also, hornets' nests, fire ants, nettles, and broken bottles. She gave me a pair of her work gloves and said that if I found any wild sunflowers, to let her know. She'd like to cut them for a vase.

"Mom," I said, turning to her, "ask Dad what cowmint looks like."

"Josh," she said, smiling down at me, "you can ask him yourself."

"Mom, *please*," I said, giving my feet a little stomp.

She gave me her unhappy look, shook her head, then stepped over to the bathroom door.

"Bill, your son has a question for you," she called through the shut door.

I cringed down at what she was about to put me through. A second later, my father's head popped out from behind the door. His face was covered with shaving cream, and steam spilled through the door around him.

"What?" he said, looking down at me, then farther down at my hands, seeing the brown cotton work gloves I had on and Mom's little blue garden shovel in my grip.

"Go on," said my mother. "Ask, Josh."

"I'm waiting here, dammit," he growled.

"What's cowmint look like?" I asked.

He turned to Mom with a frown that made the shaving cream ripple on his face like drifting snow.

"Katie, I'm trying to get ready for work here. Do you mind?"

"Oh, Bill, please."

He looked down at me again.

"Crazy nonsense. That damn Niles. I don't know—you'll know it when you see it, Josh. Now go away. Katie, can I have some damn privacy here?"

He shut the door. I turned to Mom, finding a bright smile on her face.

"There," she said, moving me away from the door, "you'll know it when you see it."

I followed her back out onto the porch. She already had on a pair of work gloves of her own this morning and had been up earlier than me, refinishing an old chair on the back porch. Our big visit with Mr. Richmond last night had her excited, too. My mother loved antiques, and Mr. Richmond was an inspiration. There was a glow on her face, and her arms moved fast as she went back to sanding the chair legs.

"Mr. Richmond's pretty amazing, isn't he?" I said.

She stopped and looked up at me.

"Well, don't forget your father. He came up with the plant in the first place." She gave the chair leg a few more strokes with the sandpaper, then stopped and looked up again. "Okay?"

"I know," I said.

She went on sanding.

"Yes, Mr. Richmond's 'amazing,'" she finally said, rolling her eyes.

After a moment, she stopped and looked up at me again.

"Well, what are you waiting for?"

I turned and headed back out into the weeds, kicking and sorting my way through as Dad used to. I found tiny blue flowers hiding inside clumps of knifelike grass, white powder-puff balls that exploded into dust when I touched them, and silver leaves that smelled like cucumbers. Some time later, Luke came running over in a bright-yellow shirt that fit right in with the tops of buttercups.

"Did your father really cure someone with that plant?" he asked, all out of breath.

Just when I nodded as smugly as I could, I saw him overdoing a smile, as if happy for me that I had found a reason to like my mean father.

I wasn't feeling sorry for myself anymore, and he knew it. So why couldn't he be jealous of that, instead of all happy for me for having some silly reason to admire my father? Just like that, he seemed to steal the moment away from me.

As I let him search for cowmint with me, I waited for him to say something good about my parents' visit last night, that his father admired my father and liked my mother, but all he said was that he and his brothers ended up watching the remake of *King Kong* at the Fredericktown Mall and didn't get home until almost midnight. It seemed rude to me that he had forgotten about our visit in the first place. I ended up with the feeling that he and his brothers had actually avoided being home, on account of my brothers. I wouldn't have been surprised.

We continued searching, pushing bushy plants this way, that way, peering behind them, as if looking for presents behind a hundred little Christmas trees. But soon nothing looked special. Even with Dad's field guide, we couldn't tell one plant from the other, except maybe honeysuckle from dandelions. We did find violets and something that looked like a gourd. Mostly I found our old toys—part of a plastic flute, the soccer ball Jerry had poked a hole in, a half-rotted Nerf ball, and a regular baseball that I didn't recognize or remember.

Soon Luke was bored. He wandered a few feet away and stood looking up at the church steeple on the far side of my house. I stopped and looked up with him. It was so high over us that the gold cross on the tip was like a shimmering rocket soaring into outer space. We followed the steeple down with our eyes, and down, and down, until it stomped down on the far side of our house like the leg of a giant, shaking the ground.

"Is it Father Ron's church that owns your grandmother's old house?" he asked out of the blue.

When I nodded, his eyes went crazy with excitement.

"Hey, maybe those stolen church things are in there!" he said, pointing at the steeple. "Let's go look!"

I had to grab him by the arm to stop him from marching out of the lot and down the sidewalk to St. Peter's.

"Stolen items in a church?" I said. "That's totally dumb."

We went back to searching for cowmint, but that didn't stop Luke from spouting off more stupid ideas. We could organize a search for the stolen church belongings, he said—create a message board, put an ad in the local paper, contact the police.

"Hey, maybe somebody's trying to sell them on eBay!"

I stood grinning and shaking my head. Talk about imagination! Never mind that everything had been stolen years ago.

I wanted to look for cowmint—no, more than that—I was determined to look for cowmint. But all Luke wanted to talk about were candles and crucifixes buried in the plaster walls of my grandmother's old house. Treasures just waiting for us to dig out, he said.

"Hey, you think Ricky knows anything?" He turned and started toward his house. "Let's ask him."

"No, don't!"

Luke stopped.

"Why not?" he said, looking me up and down. "He's your cousin, isn't he?"

I wasn't sure how to answer him. Being from Boston, Luke just didn't understand. In West Virginia, there were cousins, and there were *cousins*. Some were why everybody in Maryland and Virginia thought West Virginia was full of hillbillies. Ricky was definitely one.

I went on searching, but Luke stood eyeing me.

"How's Ricky related to you all?" he asked.

"I don't know. Just some cousin," I said.

"You don't know?" He folded up his skinny arms. "Is he a first or second cousin?"

I shrugged.

"Why don't you know?" he asked, grinning at me as if I were the weirdest kid in the world.

I didn't want to shrug again, so I didn't answer him at all.

Just because we all lived in the same house didn't mean we talked about things. And just because my relatives all lived in the same county didn't mean they got along either.

I turned and asked Luke a question for a change.

"Why in the world did your dad ever hire Ricky?"

It felt good speaking up for a change, standing there with my nose all wrinkled up, like Luke's.

"Father Ron recommended him," he said.

I stood wide-eyed.

"He recommended him?" I said.

Luke nodded as if it was no big deal, but it didn't make any sense to me. Father Ron recommending Ricky Hardaway? It must have been through some charity, because Ricky hung around with the worst characters and lived in a shack somewhere along the river. I couldn't picture him ever setting foot in church for any other reason besides a free lunch or a handout.

Suddenly, something zinged overhead, tearing through the trees. Luke and I stopped and stood looking up and all around. A second later, something again zipped through the trees above us, smacking through the leaves. It sounded like rocks being thrown at us, only faster and smaller than rocks. Then I figured it out—*Jerry was shooting his BB gun at us!*

"Get down!" I yelled.

Luke and I dropped flat in the weeds.

"Is he trying to hit us?" Luke whispered, his face all scrunched-up scared.

I shook my head. Jerry was a total jerk, but he wouldn't shoot us.

"He's just trying to scare us," I said, peering around like a soldier.

We stayed crouched down in the weeds for some time as BBs whizzed all around us—whistling through the leaves, zipping off stumps, striking rocks, flying here and there. Luke looked scared to death.

"He's crazy!" he hissed.

Then, as suddenly as it started, the BBs stopped, and it was quiet again. I rose up slowly, peering all around. For sure, Jerry was still lurking out there somewhere, enjoying terrorizing us.

With my brother, the Mad Sniper, on the loose, Luke wanted to go back over to his house to see if any of my ancestors in the old house along the river were in this book his father had on ghosts of Harpers Ferry, but I wanted to go on searching for cowmint. Instead, we ended up in the trees near the front of my house, where Jerry knew better than to shoot at us, since Mom would hear him through the kitchen window.

The front porch was the only decent part of our house. Up here, as long as the welcome mat was in place, the concrete didn't look so cracked up, and the porch columns weren't so blistered and flaking. Luke and I sat on the bench, where we could see tourists through the overhanging trees. Only they couldn't see us back. Dad had arranged the trees this way, letting them grow and trimming them ever so slightly.

"Hey, watch this," I said.

I crept through the trees to where daylight began to flicker beyond, then put my hands to my mouth like a bullhorn.

"Psst! Hey, fatso!" I hissed through the trees to the street.

Luke and I doubled over and held back our laughs as the fat man on the sidewalk stopped and looked around for whoever had just called him that name.

"Psst! Hey, blubber butt!" I hissed again through the camouflage of trees.

Again, the red-faced angry man looked all around, left, then right, wondering who on the street was calling him these names.

Luke crept up beside me.

"And they can never see you in here?" he whispered, looking at me in amazement.

I shook my head, a smug glow on my face.

"Never," I said.

We sat and peered out at the crowds of rich tourists from the city who could never see our house inside the trees.

"It's like you all live on an island," Luke said, looking around at the spotty tent of maples over my house.

I looked around with him, happy to have a friend for once under this tent with me. Suddenly I wasn't so bothered by it all: the rusted gutters hanging down on the side of our house, the mud wasp nests looking like slop thrown against the upper windows, the horseflies swarming around us like hornets, hitting our bare arms, everything looking so creepy and rickety.

"Hey, you're King Kong on a deserted island," he said.

I felt a pang inside, thinking of myself as a big angry ape hidden in the middle of Harpers Ferry. I didn't want to be King Kong in Harpers Ferry. I wanted to be Thomas Jefferson or Abe Lincoln.

"You ever go down in town?" he asked.

I shook my head.

"What? You're kidding?" he said.

"Not in the summer," I said. "Because of all the tourists."

He sat looking at me, and looking at me.

"Come on," he said. "Let's go."

"No way. Dad'll kill me."

"You wanna go to art school in the city someday, right?"

I nodded.

"Well, you can't hide under the trees like King Kong then."

A grin crept over his face, and before I knew it, he was yanking on my arm, and I was following him through the trees—breaking through the tent over my house and crashing into the sunlit street, in front of hundreds and hundreds of tourists!

CHAPTER VI: ESCAPE!

K ING KONG BOY BREAKS FREE—RAAARR!" Luke roared at the startled tourists on the sidewalk, causing some lady to spill her Coke.

We took off to the far side of the street, our sneaks clapping down on the pavement as we came to a stop at the big picture window with John Brown in it. Luke was gaping up, all wowed out of his mind, even though he had seen it before. Tourists were gathered around under the window, grinning and pointing up at the crazy-looking figure: Brown, the wild-looking giant, with bulging eyes and long brown hair and a bloodstained bandage around his head.

"Oh, hey, guess what?" Luke turned to me. "I almost forgot. Dad's gonna be John Brown in the big town play!" he said.

My eyes went as wide as his.

"Your dad's gonna be John Brown in the play?"

"Yeah! He just found out. It'll be great." He turned and looked up at the wax figure of Brown as if to tell him, too. "Alex, Daniel, and I are supposed to have parts, too."

Every August, the park people who lived in the fancy houses on the hill put on a play about John Brown's famous trial for treason and held it in one of their nice houses. My family was never invited. Afterward, there were pictures and write-ups in all the papers. Mom was always curious about it, but Dad said he'd rather use the newspaper articles to put his wet boots on.

But Mr. Richmond playing John Brown? First of all, he was too short. He wasn't much taller than my mother. More than that, he was so kind and full of smiles. He'd make a great Ben Franklin, or Santa Claus, or even Gepetto, but never John Brown.

As I gazed up at this crazy-looking Brown, I tried to imagine Mr. Richmond looking so angry. I never knew who played John Brown the years before in the big play, but he had to be somebody who already looked mean. If my father grew a beard, he'd be John Brown easy.

Luke hopped up on the railing to gawk up at his idol.

"He was a Kansas Jayhawker," he said. "He burned twenty-two farms between Missouri and Virginia in three days."

"Twenty-two!"

"Yeah, but they all deserved it," he said. "They all owned slaves."

"Oh."

I stood glancing up and down the street at the hundreds of tourists I usually hid from whenever I was this close to my embarrassing house. I looked down at my cruddy jeans, which I didn't like the snooty tourists seeing, then back at my house, which never looked hidden enough. I didn't have to wonder whether John Brown would burn down my house. There was still one slaveholder left in the world. Dad!

Luke turned and followed John Brown's eyes across the street.

"Hey, he's looking right at your house!" he said, as if we were the luckiest people in the world.

Tell me about it.

Then Luke reached up under the big picture window and pushed the little worn button beside a tiny speaker, and, a second later, an important-sounding voice started speaking: "John Brown. Who was he? A saint? A madman?"

"A saint," said Luke to the tiny speaker.

"No, a madman," I said, grinning, just to tease Luke.

He spun around, glaring at me.

"Clouds hung low over the heights above town . . .," the voice continued.

Luke stood listening to every word, as if we were in history class or something. Suddenly, he cried out, "Hey, what's that?"

I watched as he hopped off the railing, reached up to the big window, and ran his finger over a tiny hole in the glass, just below John Brown's belt buckle, where you didn't want to be pointing in broad daylight.

"It's a BB hole!" he cried out, whirling around and frowning at me.

I tried to look innocent, but the guilt was on my face. Over the years, my brothers had shot, thrown, and spit everything they could think of at this picture window, like it was a carnival dunking machine and John Brown was the target. You almost felt sorry for John Brown, taking the heat for our father; my brothers couldn't shoot, throw, or spit anything at him, but they could at his twin.

"And what the heck are these?" Luke went on, feeling his hand over tiny scratches in the glass, made from years of gravel-packed snowballs Jerry had chucked at this big window.

I didn't say a word, and we stood looking up at Brown for a few more minutes. Then we took off down the street, past souvenir shop after souvenir shop—The Jackboot, The Jeb Stuart Gift Shop, The Belle of Appomattox.

"Hey, remember the other day?" Luke said, stopping to point at a doorway. "Go away, ghost!" He ran a little farther, then stopped and pointed at the next door. "Go away, ghost!"

He had me laughing my head off by the time we reached the bottom of the hill, at Potomac Street. Potomac Street was like a Hollywood movie set of the Civil War. There was a B. J. Blum's Dry Goods store, with watermelons and burlap sacks lining the slate walk in front. Next to it was McKenzie's Confectionary, its pink-curtained windows filled with jars of green and red striped candy sticks. There was even an old-time post office with a horse trough in front, brimful with clear water, a bright Confederate flag waving lazily in the breeze.

Luke had his eyes on the blacksmith shop, so we dashed inside. The stone walls were high and soot-covered, and the huge fireplaces were so stained with coal they looked like blackened mouths living in the rock. Working the bellows were park people dressed up as blacksmiths, wearing choo-choo train hats and heavy cotton coveralls and having brawny forearms as they pumped big orange flames high into the air. Luke leaned over the railing as far as he could, to feel the heat from the fires. Then, as quickly as we dashed in, we dashed out.

"That's our bus stop," I told him, pointing at the green park bench in front of the shop.

Bus #72, my school bus, came right through the old-time park and stopped here.

"Wait," said Luke, looking at me. "You saying we catch the bus in front of"—he turned to read the shop sign—"the 'Garrison Lee Blacksmith Shop. Established 1859'?"

When I nodded, he yelled out like a fool—"Yes!" And we took off running again.

Clacking up and down the cobblestone street were horse-drawn carriages with candy-apple red wheels, and riding on top were men in Abe Lincoln stovepipe hats and women in blue bonnets. Crossing the street were ladies in red-checkered hoop dresses that looked blown up like hot-air balloons. On the brick walk stood Civil War soldiers, their long blue legs decorated with shiny metal swords and jackboots long enough to hide our whole arms in. Out on the green, beyond a split-rail fence, were more soldiers, holding long flaming torches and firing cannons that sat on stout, shiny-black wagon wheels.

Ba-BOOM! Ba-BOOM! Ba-BOOM!

Smelly black powder smoke poured over the grass as

echoes of cannon fire clapped up the skeleton-white rock face of the mountain across the river, only to split, crackle, and roll like thunder around the bushy-green mountains to our rear, then come boomeranging down into town again, causing heads to shrink down as if the skies were falling. Luke and I were grinning like crazy, along with the rest of the crowd, our grins as big as dinner plates, our oohs and aahs fizzling out like fireworks.

When the cannon firing was over, we took off down to John Brown's Fort, to pretend we were John Brown and his raiders around the patched-up, faded brick firehouse, which was surrounded by wood-chip trails and brown park markers. Everywhere were tourists shaped and colored like circus balloons. But for once, I didn't care whether they gawked at my short hair and cruddy jeans or whether they called me a local yokel to themselves. I was with Luke. He wasn't gawking at me, and he looked like them. So why should they?

"Charge!" we roared, running through them as the sword-drawing ghosts of John Brown and his Kansas raiders, dashing madly down a wood-chip trail until breaking free onto the riverbank, our sneaks quickly filling up with yellow sand. Laughing, firing our rifles here and there, we followed the wood-chip trail back under the train trestles, stopping to look at bubbles of creosote oozing from the trestle timbers, like a Hershey's bar melting in the sun. Luke stuck his finger in the black gunk, then tried to wipe it on me. I bayoneted him and ran away.

When he caught up with me, we crept alongside the Master Armorer's House and peered in windows filled with gold-trimmed muskets. With Luke going first, we dashed inside to air-conditioning and fell in behind a school group. The park ranger at the head of the group was speaking in a loud voice. Around the room were crisscrossing pistols under bright glass, along with small models of water-powered factories. Luke and I leaned close to a glass case and grinned at the million moving parts—gears turning, levers pumping.

From here, we dashed through the gift shop, out the back door, across the street, and into a souvenir shop, the bell over the door dinging. Inside was a mess of souvenirs—flags, toy muskets, books, coffee cups, a ton of junk. I waited for the old lady behind the cash register to look up, recognize me as a Connors boy, and frown, even though it was Jerry who had shoveled snow up against her door last winter, just to see her stand there helpless when she tried to open her shop in the morning. But when she did look up, she saw Luke's face first, along with his combed-out sissy-boy brown hair and his bright-yellow shirt. He looked like a tourist, and she smiled. And her smile was already on her face when she saw me. I wondered if she had seen me at all, or whether Luke was a blur in her eyes when she looked at me. Funny how people start all over with you when you're beside the right person.

I was impressed that Luke knew how to look around at souvenirs like a tourist. He walked slowly past the shot glasses, rebel flags, and toy revolvers, looking down as if seriously considering buying something. He spun the postcard rack. He even stopped and carefully picked up something.

"May I help you?" the old lady said, with the same smile.

"How much is this?" Luke asked, holding up a Civil War cannon pencil sharpener.

"Two ninety-nine."

"Thank you."

He put it down and moved on. I was completely impressed. I had been living here all my life, and I hadn't said two words to this lady, much less set foot in this shop, or any shop.

Back out on Shenandoah Street, we heard church bells clanging and looked up to see the gold cross of St. Peter's shining in the blue sky. We'd almost come full circle, down the street and up again. Below, tourists were filing into the big archway.

"Come on!" Luke cried out. "We can check it out for stolen items."

Up the hill we dashed, passing tourists. At the top of the Stone Steps, I grabbed Luke's arm.

"I can't," I said.

He stood looking back at me.

"Why not?"

"'Cause I haven't been to confession."

His face scrunched up. "Confession?"

It was hard to explain. When you're Catholic and you miss mass—and I had missed three years' worth, not to mention attending Christmas Eve mass at a Methodist church—you have to go to confession before you can go to mass again. It was a rule. Luke, though, not being Catholic, could go anytime he wanted. I didn't mention that my father had forbidden me to step foot in St. Peter's.

Luke turned and pointed to the tourists pouring into the church.

"What about all of them? They're going. Come on!"

I watched as he took off without me. Maybe he was right. I quickly caught up with him where Father Ron was greeting everyone as they went through the big archway. As Luke and I passed, he gave us both a smile and a nod. He was young, big-shouldered, and looked hot, dressed all in black.

"Wow!" Luke whispered, once we were inside, gaping around at all the flickering candles and stained-glass windows, then peering up at the superhigh, fancy ceiling.

He wanted to sit up front near the altar, but I didn't want anyone seeing me in here and having it getting back to Dad. So Luke finally gave in, and we sat in the rear pew, where we looked all around.

The church sure had changed since I had been in here three years ago. It was all-white now, and the flicker of red, blue, and yellow candles around the altar made me think of a birthday cake. Gone were the scary bloody images of Christ stabbed and dying on the cross, and in their place were simple modern ones that almost looked made for kids. In the big stained-glass window behind the altar, the image of Christ had a silly smile. The organ was playing a lively tune, like the old-time calliope at the county fair, and over by the confessional was a white neon sign. I couldn't believe what it said—ADMIT ONE.

Admit One? Like in a movie theater? Wow, no wonder Dad didn't like Father Ron. He *was* liberal.

Sitting in the pew, glancing back at the confessional, I remembered when I went to confession while Father Zimmer was the priest. Dad told me beforehand just what I had to say. It was awful. The dark drapes of the confessional swallowed me up, and I was alone with a priest as strict as my father. My voice squeaked and squawked as I confessed rehearsed sins: not listening to my father, causing fights with my brothers, making life hard on my mother. All lies. I sobbed and made a horrible spectacle of myself inside the confessional, and Father Zimmer only made it worse. In the pitch black, his deep voice bore down on me through the screen. I thought he was the devil. It was an awful, awful memory. I was glad I would never have to go to confession again.

When the organ music stopped, lights rose around the pews, and Father Ron came out from behind a black curtain to the right of the altar. He gave a cheerful wave to everyone.

"Hello, my friends!" he called out far and wide.

He strolled up the center aisle, shaking every hand he could, to the left, to the right, like a politician. Luke, closer to the aisle than me, got to shake his hand before I did. When he turned and started back down the aisle, his black robe swung apart in back. I couldn't believe it—he was wearing blue jeans and Hush Puppies!

Then he stopped in the middle of the aisle, turned, and smiled all around.

"What do you call a nun who walks in her sleep?" he asked.

From pew to pew, heads turned, and smiles flickered like candles.

"A roaming Catholic. Come on, folks, you all should know that one by now," he said, turning and walking on.

Chuckling broke out all over, and Luke and I sat grinning our heads off. A joke in church? This didn't seem like mass at all. It was like a show or something.

Then we all stood and started reading from prayer books kept in slots behind the pews. Only there weren't enough to go around, so Luke and I shared one. Luke, not being Catholic, was full of stupid questions. Do we sing? Was the prayer book like a small Bible? What did the short passages in Latin mean? I pretended I knew all the answers, but it had been a long time since I had been to mass. Soon I kept losing my place as we read along. I even fudged it by mumbling and repeating whatever the lady in front of me said a split second after she said it. Dad always said my brothers' and my biggest problem in life was not knowing the liturgy. Hard to believe he ever said that.

After sitting, standing, and kneeling half a dozen times, we got to sit back for a while as Father Ron talked about a church bake sale that had been moved up a week, renovations on the bell tower that were to begin next month, and a yearly sacrament meeting to be held in the fall.

I sat looking around. I couldn't get over how much church had changed—tourists in shorts, part of the ceiling painted baby blue. I even saw a Pioneer stereo speaker mounted to the altar that Jerry would love to blast his music over, and near one Station of the Cross was a small wooden sign carved in Old Testament letters that used to read: NO MAN HATH SEEN GOD. Now it said, NO DRINKS OR FOOD ALLOWED IN CHURCH. Dad, if he caught me in here, and after blistering my butt if he did, would say I was hanging out with the damn Episcopalians!

Church had changed on the inside, too. No blaming. No kids with their heads hung low, hearing awful stories—purgatory was the story I could never bear. For years, mean-faced Father Zimmer had stood glaring down at us like Dad in a robe, telling us how much we had sinned. But Father Ron talked to us like a kindergarten teacher. He even told us about his two Dalmatians, a fishing trip he took to Maine, and the cost of aluminum siding for his house in Middleton. I wasn't sure whether this was better—maybe Dad was right for once; maybe the church had lost something—but what I knew for sure was that I felt better being here.

Chapter VII: THE FACE IN THE WINDOW

I T WAS THE NEXT DAY before I continued my search for cowmint, working my way back across the weedy lot. I found sunflowers being circled by bumblebees, ferns with sawtooth edges to their leaves, and white petals so curled up they looked like little trumpets you could blow. Suddenly a voice called out, "Hey, up here." I looked up into the trees, the sunlight pouring through my fingers, and hanging from a branch and grinning down at me was Ricky Hardaway!

"Hey, cous," he called down, smiling his chipped-up teeth at me.

He dropped to the ground and stood there with no shirt on, grinning. In the sunlight, his muscles looked big and copper. Both arms were streaked with paint, and fine pebbles were stuck to his shoulders. Matted in his long, stringy hair were twigs—and what looked like bubble gum. *Bubble gum?* He had tattoos all over his body. A cigarette was smoldering from his fingertips—or at least I thought it was a cigarette. He stood towering over me, staring down at me like I was a runt.

I knew from Luke that he was still working on the top floors of the Richmonds' house, spackling and painting, and I guessed from the McDonald's wrappers on the ground he was on his lunch break. I could only hope he wouldn't push me around, since I was friends with Luke and he worked for Luke's father. Jerry said he had failed the eighth grade so many times he was no longer a minor when they expelled him for good for stabbing a boy right in the classroom. Since then, he had been in and out of Moundsville Correctional Institute more times than you could keep track of.

"What in the hell ya doin'?" he asked me.

He went on grinning at me, showing a green front tooth, yellow lower teeth, and something black and silver on the side.

"Looking for cowmint," I said.

"Cowshit! Looking for cowshit!" he shouted. "Well, don't get none on your fingers, boy!"

I found myself actually grinning back. He was gross but funny. I wasn't as scared of him as I was supposed to be.

"It's a miracle plant," I said, whether I believed it or not.

He came closer and leaned down.

"Miracle plant?"

At once I was hypnotized by his big scar. It looked like a train had wrecked into his forehead and just bounced off, leaving a dead eye that made half of him look like a robot. On top of that, he had a big grape-colored birthmark on his neck, and on his shoulder was a Metallica Rocks tattoo. He made no effort to hide the smelly joint he was smoking.

He shot his muscular arm down at me.

"Well, hell, if you find some, tell me. I could use a miracle."

I couldn't take my eyes off his chin whiskers, which were as thick as horsehair.

As bad luck would have it at that moment, Dad's car pulled up to our house. Ricky, seeing it, gave me a friendly slap on the back, then scampered off toward the Richmonds' house. Dad, getting out of the car in a hurry, stood glaring across the yard at him, then started waving me over to the house.

My father was yelling by the time I reached the house.

"Katie, that damn kid of yours is tearing up my backyard!"

He was in another foul mood. He usually was after work.

Mom was on the back porch, sweeping. "Oh, let him look, Bill," she said.

"Let him look? Let him look! For that damn plant? For something that doesn't exist?"

When he popped out a laugh, she turned around, broom in hand.

"No, for something you 'made up,'" she said.

I made the mistake of trying to sneak past him, and he grabbed me by the arm.

"You're not to talk about your grandmother's house over there, buster," he growled. "You hear me?"

I leaned as far away from him as I could.

"Bill, please," said my mother, hurrying across the porch.

"Katie, I don't want him talking about the old Marist retreat over at that house," he said. He turned to me and yanked me by the arm again. "You keep your mouth shut about that place, buster."

I broke free and escaped around behind my mother, then into the kitchen, where I ran into Jerry, who was helping himself to a Suzy Q from the box on top of the fridge.

"It's full of bums," he said.

Dad pointed through the screen door at him.

"It better not be—and you stay the hell away from there." He pointed at Robbie, too, who was sitting at the table, his fat face already devouring a Suzy Q. "All of you all. This is the last time I'm telling you. That house is no damn playhouse!"

My brothers and I stood staring out at him, never understanding why Grandma's old house made him so crazy.

"Bill, please, lower your voice," my mother said, looking around.

"Josh, come back out here," he said, pointing his finger down at the porch. "I'm not finished with you."

My brothers laughed, as I would get backhanded for sure now. When I stepped through the squeaky screen door, Dad leaned down in my face. I could see his bristly nose hairs, as if he had snorted up a wire brush. I could see, too, his roughed-up red skin, like he wiped his face with sandpaper. I could smell his pipe tobacco breath and count every ugly short hair on his head.

"What was that damn boy saying to you over there?" he said, pointing back across our yard.

"Who, Bill?" said my mother, trying to wedge herself between us. "Luke?"

"No, that damn Ricky!" he snapped.

"Nothing," I said, my voice trembling as I leaned bow-backed away from him.

"Don't say 'nothing,' buster. You two were talking about something over there. I saw you." He leaned down in my face again. "Now I wanna know every word that was said!"

"Bill, please."

"Katie, stay out of this."

"Nothing, Dad!" I cried out. "I just told him about cowmint."

Jerry burst out laughing behind me. Robbie, too.

"Ricky'll try to smoke it!" Jerry howled out.

When Dad stood up straight and turned to Mom, I made my escape to the far side of the porch.

"Katie, I told that damn Niles that hiring Ricky was a mistake, but he wouldn't listen."

"He sneaks out to Grandma's old house," said Jerry through the screen door.

Dad whirled around. "How in the hell you know that?"

"He and Snake Wilson smoke dope up in that top room," Jerry went on.

Mom's face twisted up in alarm. Dad's turned blueberry. Snake Wilson! He made two of Ricky Hardaway, as far as being bad. Everybody in town knew Snake Wilson ran over his stepfather with a lawn tractor.

"No, you smoke dope up there," Robbie said, lobbing a banana off the table at Jerry but hitting the screen door instead.

"Oh, Jerry, you know that for sure?" Mom asked, quickly stepping between him, the screen door, and our father, before Dad could blow a gasket.

"No, hell, Katie, he doesn't know anything for sure," Dad muttered, turning to catch sight of me running away. "Stay the hell out of those weeds!"

"'I'll know it when I see it'!" I yelled over my shoulder.

"And I wanted to be a sea captain at one time!" he yelled back, pulling out an ugly old joke between us.

I dashed back over to the vacant lot and went on kicking weeds apart, finding mustard-colored flowers with berries that looked like black jelly beans. I thought about my father once wanting to become a sea captain. For the longest time, whenever he said this, I believed him. I'd imagine him on a ship, turning the big wheel, the waves splashing over him. It was exciting to think of him no longer riding around in our old car all day, delivering mail and collecting rubber bands on the gearshift. But whenever I got excited for him in this way, he would just shake his head at me, as if I was the dumbest kid in the world. Mom said he was being sarcastic. He should have *never wanted* to be a sea captain, was what he meant. When I asked him why, he was quick to tell me that just because a person wanted something didn't mean he had the right to want it. He said this as if trying to teach me one of the Ten Commandments. But I understood this even less, and he said that was because Mom had spoiled me. Still, I knew it was better to be spoiled than not to want to be a sea captain.

Angry, I reached down and yanked up a clump of weeds, the dirt from the roots spraying all over my sneaks. I held the plant up and looked at it from all angles. Dull leaves, limp stem. No, there was nothing special about it. I tossed it back into the weeds, as if throwing a fish back into the river.

I wasn't sure why I then started marching back to the house, empty-handed. When I stepped up on my porch, I saw my father through the kitchen window, looking at my mother in a way I had never seen before. The yellow kitchen light made his face look like wax, only sad-looking, as if one of us had died and he was telling Mom about it.

I put my ear close to the screen window as he sat down at the kitchen table.

"Katie, you know what that damn fellow did today? He went out there and started poking around that old house," he said.

Mom turned from the stove.

"Who? What old house?"

"Niles Richmond. Who do you think? My mom's old house, down on River Road—would you listen, dammit?"

Mom started over to the table, the soup spoon in her hand dripping.

"*Niles* went out to your mother's old house?" she asked, wide-eyed.

"Today, yes," he said.

Behind the screen window, I stood just as amazed as my mother. Mr. Richmond poking around the white house?

Mom quickly sat down at the table with my father, the big soup spoon disappearing on her lap.

"Good heavens, why, Bill?"

Dad was staring off into space. "I don't know *why*, Katie." Then he looked at her, his eyes bloodshot from the day. "All your damn son's crazy talk the other night probably. Made him curious." He sat back in the crackly cane chair and looked off again. "He even called the courthouse and asked about the deed to the house."

"Called the court—"

"Stopped by the post office today to tell me so," he said, leaning forward, his big arms coming unfolded. "Like I'd be pleased or something." He stared at her for a moment. "And you know what they told him?"

"That the church owned it?" she said.

"Of course that the church owns it! I told him that myself."

He sat back and stared off into nowhere again. My mother looked down at the table and started pressing out wrinkles in the pink tablecloth.

"Bill, I think it's just normal curiosity," she said.

"*Normal curiosity*, hell. That place is none of his business. It's nobody's business."

"He's a park historian. I suppose he thinks it is his business to know."

"It's not park land. It's not his business."

He sat with a sullen, stubborn face until it was my mother's turn to cross her arms.

"Bill, you *must* speak with someone about this," she said.

"No," he said. "No, no, no."

"Maybe even confession," she said, touching his sleeve.

"Confession!" he cried out.

I snapped my head back from the window screen. *Confession?* Dad going to confession?

Back when we still went to church, my brothers and I were the ones always told to go to confession. We were bad, not Dad. I peered through the screen. What had my father done?

"Speak to that flake Father Ron!" he shot back, getting redder in the face. "Hell, no."

"Bill," she said, pointing in the direction of the church, "that man over there is not who you think he is."

My face was pressed against the window screen. Who did my father think Father Ron was?

Mom stood up and leaned over the table at my father.

"Bill, this will follow you for the rest of your life. Deal with it. Look at what it's doing to you right now. You go crazy whenever your son brings up that old house." She swung her arm back and very nearly pointed at the window where I was crouched. "No wonder he keeps talking about it. He *senses* something."

"*Senses* hell. He's just nosy—and never listens. And he's too damn busy with those colored pencils of his. Too busy daydreaming!" He pointed his finger at her. "Katie, you were the one who wanted to have another kid. Two was damn plenty enough for me. I told you—"

"Shh!" she said, glancing all around.

Ducking down, I could feel myself freezing up inside. *What was following him? What was I sensing?*

Peering in again, I saw my father's shoulders fall. For the longest while, he sat staring off with that zombie look my brothers got whenever they had been sneaking out to Grandma's house, drifting in and out of the empty rooms. Then, under the dim kitchen light, I saw a glisten in his eyes.

Tears? I stepped back from the window. Was my father crying?

Mom creaked forward in her chair, with even more strain on her face, with even more veins in her forehead, and with even more of a whittled look to her nose.

"Oh, Bill," she said.

I couldn't believe what I was seeing. My father never cried.

I QUICKLY BACKED UP FROM the window and hurried out into the yard. *My father crying?* I couldn't get it out of my head—his face looked like the wax bust of John Brown across the street melting in a fire!

My mind started flipping and tumbling. What was following my father? Spooky shadows followed me at night. That was scary. Mom said a weight problem would follow Robbie all his life. Bad grades followed Jerry. Sometimes that made him cry.

I started kicking the weeds harder than ever, trying to beat the secrets out of them. I booted a rusted can high into the air. Who did my father think Father Ron was? I thought as hard as I could, but all I could come up with was Lee Jackson, the richest jerk in town. But that made no sense. He and Father Ron were nothing alike.

I pulled a big rock aside, and ants spilled out. They ran in every direction, like thieves.

Thieves. Whoever stole the silver statues and ivory altar figures from the Catholic retreat—that followed my father. But everything upset my father! Thankless job. Brat sons. Crowded tourist town to live in. Worst of all, we lived beside the biggest Catholic church around, a national landmark with a fancy vaulted ceiling—but we didn't go to church anymore?

Excuse me? What was wrong with this picture? The church was all around us. Even in these cockamamie weeds, the steeple next door was casting its long shadow over me like the creepy beanpole man. I couldn't take a step without stepping into the shadow like quicksand, or an oil slick. How in the world could any of these plants grow here anyway? They should all be dead from no sunlight! If not cast across this lot, the shadow was laying across our roof, making it rust and mold. Everywhere was the shadow of the church!

I pushed over another big rock, then flung aside a half-rotten fence picket, only to pick it up and use it to start whacking weeds.

I remembered when we stopped going to church. A few years back, Father Zimmer died of pneumonia one December. By January we had Father Ron. Dad hated him right away. He actually got up and left during the first sermon. Father Ron was a "damn liberal." End of story. The church became off-limits to us, along with everything else in town.

Soon after, Dad began stacking as much junk in the yard between our house and the church as he could—lawn chairs, trash cans, flowerpots, bicycle tires, broken bricks, even a fiberglass canoe—as if preparing for World War III. He even planted a poplar tree because it was fast-growing. The towering stone side of St. Peter's soon disappeared from our view, along with half the street. And ever since, leaves had been climbing over our house like termites.

Back and forth I swung the picket against the weeds, until the rotted wood finally broke. Then I started pawing through the wild plants, the pointy leaves stinging my arms and leaving gooey green stuff on my fingers. My shoes were completely dirty. I wanted to give up, as all I had found was a dead bird full of maggots and half a dozen of Ricky Hardaway's beer cans. I reached down and looked at a plant. Green leaves, no flowers—boring. Definitely not cowmint. I looked at the next plant. Spotted leaves, half a yellow flower—still boring. Probably not cowmint. Then, suddenly, when I pulled back some high grass, a plant with the brightest green berries I'd ever seen appeared. It had fuzzy, pointed leaves and purple flowers and a stem that was square. It was beautiful! I knew immediately.

"I found it!" I cried out. "I found it."

Dad said I would know it when I saw it, and I saw it. I was sure. I had found cowmint!

CHAPTER VIII: WHAT GROWS IN THE WEEDS

THERE WERE HALF A DOZEN of these plants along the bank. I ran inside, got Mom's gardening snips, came back and cut one off, then hurried back into the house with it, careful not to let the berries fall off. Dad was watching TV, and Mom was in the kitchen. When he saw me coming in with a plant in my hand, he pointed his arm toward the door like a spear.

"Get! Don't you track dirt all over this house, buster."

I stood looking at him.

"But it's cowmint, Dad," I said, grinning and holding the plant out so that he could see that I hadn't dragged it in by its dirty roots.

He stood up. Not a trace of crying remained on his face, not even red eyes. You'd have thought he had never cried once in his life.

"Josh, did you cut up my good barberry bush?" As he came over, I braced for the worst. But when he leaned down, his angry face went blank. "No, it's not barberry." He leaned even closer. "Where'd you find this?"

Mom stopped what she was doing and came over.

"It's cowmint, Dad," I said again.

"It looks like gooseberry," he said to himself.

Mom peered down with him. "It's not nightshade, is it?"

"Wait a minute now," he said, walking over to the table with my plant. "You see these leaves?" He ran his finger over one of them, then took the plant from my hand and held it up under the light. He said he had never seen needle-shaped leaves so fuzzy. Mom and I watched as he sniffed the plant and looked off as if tasting wine.

"I'll be damned."

"Bill?"

"It sure smells like a mint."

I grinned up at Mom.

"See, cowmint."

Dad smelled the plant over and over and asked me again where I'd found it. He had never seen a mint with berries, he said. Mom smelled it, too. She thought it smelled like rosemary.

"Well, is this how you remember it looking, Bill?" she asked.

"Hell, I don't know, Katie," he said. "It's been so damn long."

He started running through the mints he knew offhand—it wasn't hyssop or horehound or self-heal.

"Except for these damn berries, it looks like Montana mint."

"Montana mint? Bill, in West Virginia?"

"Dammit, Katie, I don't know what it is."

When he went to get his field guides, I went to get my sketchpad. We met back at the cowmint plant at the same time. He sat, opened a guidebook, and started glancing at photographs of plants. I sat, opened my sketchpad, and started drawing the plant I had found. Mom stood glancing at the two of us sitting side by side for once, me drawing, Dad flipping pages, both of us as busy as bees. A curious look filled her face.

Jerry and Robbie came in soon after, sweaty and rowdy from having been up to no good. They quickly sized up the situation.

"Did he find it?" Robbie asked, leaning over the plant on the table, touching the woolly leaves, then tapping the berries. "Wow, they almost look plastic."

Mom told them not to touch.

"We don't know yet," she said.

My brothers circled behind me to see my drawing. I was feverishly blending my Pine Green and Lime Green pencils to capture the berry color. Dad glanced down at my sketchpad, did a double take, but said nothing. Then he stood over the plant like a scientist, turning pages, touching and smelling leaves over and over.

"It's these berries," he said at last. "They shouldn't be here."

"*Shouldn't be,* Bill?"

Jerry stuck his big nose in.

"Crap," he said, grabbing one of the leaves and breaking it off.

That had Dad yelling and raising his hand. Mom, quickly

sending Jerry away, started sniffing the plant for herself again. It definitely smelled like basil, she said. No rosemary. Funny, she couldn't be sure.

Moments later, Robbie came back downstairs with his set of geologist loupes "borrowed" from the school's geology lab. He plucked one out of the plastic packet, held the small magnifying glass over the plant, and started examining it for himself, right in front of Dad.

"That the ten-power one?" asked my father, looking on as Robbie all but took over the examination.

"No, thirty," answered my brother, peering through the lens.

When not wearing his Rudolph the Red-Nosed Reindeer hat with yellow antlers sticking up and acting crazy like Jerry, Robbie was the smart one in the family, especially in biology and chemistry. He could mumble for hours about the periodic table, have whole conversations with himself about Zr, Au, and Fe. The problem was, he could be all earth science one minute, using terms like "soil remediation" and "homeostatic organisms," then fart at you the next.

Dad decided he wanted to see where I had found the plant, so we all traipsed outside. I showed Dad where, and sure enough, there were more plants growing along the bank. Seven in all. In the slanting evening light, the stems were fiber-optic green, the berries like Christmas lights, and the flowers, said our mother, like sapphires. My father just didn't know what to make of it. He knew field mints, but this one didn't fit.

HALF THE EVENING, he sat up with the plant, going page by page through his field guide, using Robbie's thirty-power geologist loupe. The plant actually looked closest to gooseberry, he said, except for the leaves and the fact it wasn't a shrub.

"Look at these parallel veins, Katie."

"Lanceolate? Or *ob*-lanceolate?" she said, reading from the guide.

"Katie," he said, "it sure looks like oblanceolate to me."

Which basically meant that the leaf, according to its veins, should have been shaped like a bullet, instead of like a church steeple.

I sat between Mom and Dad, with one hand holding open the pages of his field guide for him and with the other drawing in my sketchpad. But it was my father I couldn't take my eyes off of. Earlier this evening, he had been crying. Sitting here now, with my cowmint plant in his hands, he was in the calmest mood I had ever seen him in.

At one point, he turned and took a long look down at the drawing of the plant I was now lazily working on.

"You've got your berries too damn green, Josh—and big, in relation to the stem."

I was startled when he tried to take my pencil and pad from me, as if he knew how to draw. As hard as I could, I jerked both of them away from him.

"Oh, shit, look at him, Katie," he said, his face souring.

I could feel my body freeze up and lean away from him. Mom had the same terrified face I did.

"Bill?" she said, sitting up.

"Katie, I was just showing him—can't I show him?" he snapped.

"Well, yes," she said.

"Josh, give me the damn pad," he said, grabbing at my hand and shaking my sweaty fingers to loosen my grip on the pencil as well.

"Bill!" my mother cried out.

Again I jerked my hand back. But not before Jerry, who was coming down the steps, saw Dad latched ahold of my hand, the pencil between us. My brother stopped, his foot hovering over a step, his face hollow-looking.

"Jerry, your father was just showing Josh how to draw," my mother called out, sounding nervous as she started to stand, then sat back down.

Dad finally got the pencil and sketchpad out of my grip. "I know a little about sketching," he grumbled. "Remember those hand-painted birdhouses I used to make right here?"

Mom didn't answer. Jerry was still frozen. And I continued to lean away from my father.

" 'The Sutler,' " Dad said to himself, half smiling, having fun with my pencil all by himself. He flicked the pencil point here and there, giving the berries a sketchy look. "'Candy Apples. Postcards. Souvenirs. *Come in and Stay*'—remember the sign, Katie?"

"I remember, yes."

Jerry stood with his eyes glued on the moment. Dad

glanced up at him, but said nothing. By now, I was totally out of body, seeing my father drawing in my sketchpad with my pencil. How could he suddenly be so comfortable with my pencil in his hand, when all my life he had slapped me with that hand?

Seconds later, Robbie came thundering down the steps.

"We had a shop in here, Dad?" he asked, heading straight for the bag of potato chips on the table and not even noticing what was happening.

"You know we did, Robbie," said Mom.

"I had a postcard stand right over here," Dad said, pointing my pencil where today everybody stacked their shoes on newspapers if it had been raining.

Meanwhile, Jerry stood eyeing me, his eyes like slits. I was a girl for sure, and my playing patty-fingers with Dad proved it.

"Postcards, posters, Johnny Reb caps," Dad went on, getting up from the table and pointing around the room.

"Goodness, I remember, Bill," Mom said, standing and smiling with him.

"A rack of T-shirts there," he said, pointing to where the sofa was now. "A barrel of Confederate flags here." He pointed to where the TV was. Where the armchair was—he couldn't remember what had been there. Shot glasses and coffee mugs maybe, he said.

Robbie's face was all lit up. Though we had known about the shop all our lives, suddenly Dad was talking about it.

"I sat there," Dad said, pointing to the trunk in the corner covered with a quilt, "behind a little antique brass cash register."

"Antique brass?" said Mom. "You sure?"

"They'd come in—" Dad cut himself off. "Oh, well, hell, I didn't sell much."

"Why?" Jerry turned and blurted out.

I was surprised my father even bothered to answer him.

"'Cause I ended up selling the same damn things as everybody else," he said. Then he looked off into space. "No, the problem was, this place was too far up the hill. Not many walked up past the church in those days. This whole hill was run-down."

"You mean, tourists just walked through our house?" asked Robbie, wrinkling up his fat nose.

"Well, we lived upstairs at the time, Robbie," said our mother, standing over beside my father. "Heavens, Bill, twenty-one, no, twenty-two years ago—has it been that long?"

"It has," Dad said, with a nod.

Mom looked around at us.

"Boys, your father had just come home from the service. I was living in Middleton at the time, working for Potomac Edison—"

"How'd you meet?" Robbie blurted out.

Mom turned to Dad, a soft, happy smile on her face. "Bill?"

"Swimming in the rivers," he said, a grin coming over his. "Your mother was a bigmouth bass coming up the Shenandoah. I was a catfish in the Potomac. We came together down there at The Point, and she nearly gobbled me up."

"Oh, Bill," Mom said, blushing.

Robbie stood grinning his shark tooth around the room. Jerry looked twice as ugly as he grinned. I couldn't believe what was happening. Dad not angry? Us talking like a family? Then I knew. All of a sudden, I knew. It was the cowmint! The magic of cowmint.

Robbie, hopping like a goof and planting his big feet on the living room floor, asked, "What was here?"

"I don't know—a cooler of Popsicles maybe," Dad said.

"Popsicles?" Jerry said, all goofy-faced.

"What was here?" asked Robbie, playing hopscotch with our living room floor.

Dad turned to see where he was standing now.

"Calendars, candles, some such damn thing."

"Here?"

Mom answered this time. "A shelf of those little Civil War cannon pencil sharpeners."

Dad shook his head. "Never sold a one."

"What about here?" asked Robbie.

Dad looked at the space for a moment. "Nothing—no, toy revolvers."

With that, he returned to the table to continue examining my plant, the little tour into our house's past over. Mom, picking up a magazine, followed Dad, flipping pages, pretending to read. I made a wide circle around both of them and this time sat at the far side of the table, where I went back to drawing. Jerry and Robbie charged into the kitchen, pushing and shoving each other for the last Suzy Q.

"Now's the time of year for building, Bill," Mom said out of the blue, with a ring in her voice.

Dad's face was perfectly still in the light of the lamp.

"It would take only a short time to put up an addition, with the boys' help," she went on.

This was my poor mother the scavenger. When I thought of how she walked softly around my father, angling to get what she wanted, I was reminded of what I had heard in church: "The meek shall inherit the earth."

"Oh, Katie, stop kicking a dead horse, will ya?" he muttered.

They had been over it. And over it. The problem with Harpers Ferry houses was that they were so old and small you couldn't build onto them using Home Depot stuff. If zoning wasn't against it, good taste was, was how Dad always put it. An addition with vinyl siding would be the easiest to build, but, on an old limestone house, the most hideous to look at. But that was all they agreed on.

"Pete Hampshire sure has a nice addition," Mom added.

"Dammit, Katie," he said, "Pete Hampshire has a prefab ranch house with flagstone siding, not a two-hundred-year-old armory worker's house made of Shenandoah Valley limestone—and with more damn problems at every turn than a man knows what to do with!"

"Wood shingles would be fine," Mom said anyway, easing her voice in.

He popped out a laugh.

"Katie," he said, "I'm surprised you're not harping to me about Ridge Street, too."

Ridge Street. What my mother really wanted, we all knew, was a house on Ridge Street, where she had grown up. Where neighbors still waved to neighbors, she always said, where houses had porch rockers, wind chimes, and bird feeders, where green porch chairs matched the shutters—which matched the cellar doors, which matched the oil tank in back, which matched the trash barrel in front, and on and on. Our mother spoke of it like poetry. No tacky souvenir shops and loud tourists up there, she said. Just clean, quiet houses, one after the other, with new cars parked close to them, and sidewalks empty in both directions. That was what our mother really wanted. She had her reasons for it, mostly her side of the family living nearby, and he had his reasons against it—mostly her side of the family living nearby.

Dad's silence on the issue of the addition was his final answer—no.

Jerry, meanwhile, had come out of the kitchen and gone over to the living room bookcase, where he stood looking up at our three or four fat-spined photo albums.

"Hey, Mom, we have any pictures of the shop?" he asked.

Mom turned to Dad.

"Bill?"

"I don't know. We might," he said. "Don't make a mess over there, buster."

Jerry took that as permission to start hauling down the

albums. Robbie joined in. Hopping up from the table, so did I. The three of us were quiet when, opening one album, we found old black-and-white pictures of Dad's side of the family. There was Granddad Connors when he was young and thin, leaning against an old-time pickup. In the hazy gray background was the white house, glowing like a ghost. The picture was dated July 1969. My brothers and I stood looking back in time.

"Who's that?" I asked, keeping my voice low as I pointed at the snapshot on the opposite page of a woman wearing a bonnet.

"'Who's that?'" said Jerry. "You idiot, that's Grandma."

"That's Grandma?"

I peered closer. Wow, she was so much younger than I remembered her. I knew she had always been mean because of growing up poor in the Depression, and that was why Dad was mean, too, but in this picture she looked happy.

"Yeah, but who's that?" Robbie asked, pointing at a black-and-white photo of a tall, thin-faced man with funny stuck-out ears. He was standing on the porch of Grandma's white house. Around him were a lot of other people, including Grandma, Granddad, Uncle Dave, and three others, including a pie-faced man I recognized.

"Hey, Father Ron," I said, smiling and pointing at him.

Jerry burst out laughing. Robbie looked at me like I had lost my mind.

"How, you idiot?" Jerry asked, pointing at the date at the bottom of the photo. "Nineteen sixty-seven, duh?"

He was right. The photo was way too old to be Father Ron. Still, the man looked just like him. At least I thought so.

"Mom, who's this?" I called out.

She stepped over and looked down over my shoulder to see where my finger was pointing.

"Oh, good lord," she said, "where did you boys find this?" She glanced back at our father. "Let's put it away, okay?"

Dad stepped up and looked down over Mom's shoulder before she could close the photo album. His face clouded up. While Jerry gawked at Dad, who was saying nothing, I looked down at the picture again.

"He *does* look just like Father Ron," I said.

"Oh, he does not, Josh," said my mother. "You're just seeing the cleric's collar. Now let's put it away."

But Jerry had his hand on the photo album, keeping it open.

"Yeah, but who's *that*, Mom?" Robbie asked again, still pointing at the tall, thin-faced man with funny stuck-out ears.

Mom looked back at Dad, a million things being said between them.

"Boys, that's your Uncle Earl," she finally said.

"That's Uncle Earl!" Jerry cried out.

Uncle Earl was not really our uncle, but another of our no-good cousins on Dad's side of the family. Long-haired good-for-nothings, Dad always called them. Uncle Earl was the worst. He was the biggest drunk. If he wasn't stumbling down the highway, trying to hitch a ride to the liquor store to get drunker, then he was standing in the doorways over in Charles Town, panhandling. Whenever we were shopping and saw him, we crossed the street just to get away from him. "Poor old soul," Mom always said.

My brothers and I gawked down at the picture. You could never tell it was Uncle Earl. The man in the picture was so clean-cut and young-looking.

"Wow, did he ever go downhill," Jerry howled out.

"Put it away now!" Dad said, raising his voice. "I'm not telling you again!"

Mom, reaching between us, closed the photo album herself, then quickly put it back up on the shelf. She put away the other albums as well.

Dad, red-faced and glowering, stepped away and stood with his back to us, looking into the corner of the room for the longest time. He took out his pipe, smacked the bowl clean, filled and lit it, blowing out long furls of blue smoke. Then he turned and, with his head down, not looking at us, stepped over to the table, where he stood puffing and looking down at my plant again. The room was silent all around him. All the while, my brothers and I, glancing at each other, were wondering why Grandma, Uncle Earl, and a priest who looked just like Father Ron were all on the porch of the white house. But in this family there was no way we could ask.

LATER THAT NIGHT, I lay in bed unable to sleep. What a day! First, me grinning at Ricky Hardaway and not getting killed. Next, my father crying. Then, finding cowmint! My mind was thinking overtime.

The priest in the photo album—who was he? Was this the man my father thought was Father Ron, just as I did when I first saw his picture?

I had to find out more. I had to look at the picture again. Quietly, I sneaked down the bunk bed ladder, then on downstairs. I found the same blue photo album on the shelf and hauled it down. I started turning pages. There among all the pictures was a big square of white. I couldn't believe it.

The picture of the strange priest was gone!

CHAPTER IX: NO, HEAVEN FORFEND!

I N THE MORNING, DAD WAS out in the weeds again with my cowmint plant between his fingers, revisiting the site of my discovery. I was quick to tag along. We stood together in the thickest part of the vacant lot, sunshine and bugs in our face, looking down at the seven other cowmint plants, which looked even taller in the morning light, as if they had grown inches overnight. Dad was shaking his head, so lost in thought he didn't turn to the chirping of a big cardinal right over his head. All around us, from the searching that went on yesterday, weeds were trampled, battered, and uprooted, the whole lot looking as if elephants had stampeded through. Dad eventually cussed at finding his good screwdriver in the dirt. He also found Ricky's cigarette butts mashed around—they better be Ricky's, he said, looking around for Jerry.

"Well," he finally said, looking at my plant in his hand, "we'll see."

He was not really talking to me, but more to himself. Mom had told me earlier that Dad knew a fellow on his mail route who might be able to identify the plant, though it could take weeks.

As I stood in the weeds, watching my father walk off to his car to go to a job he hated, I hoped my cowmint plant in his hand would help. All the while, the wax figure of John Brown stood watching from across the street. For a moment and from a certain angle, John Brown seemed to hope, too.

As soon as Dad pulled away, I stepped across the street and up to the picture window that held all six feet two inches of John Brown over the street like a glass coffin turned up on its end. The longer I stared at him, seeing the BB hole Jerry had put in the glass, along with scratches from years of gravel-packed snowballs, the more I saw in his face that same tired anger I knew so well. I wondered if he ever cried like my father, if he ever went to confession. I wondered if, in all his miles of writing poetry, delivering babies, and being a Mormon preacher, he ever picked up a wildflower, told an old lady in a wheelchair it was valuable, and watched her stand and use her legs like a miracle. If I could reach through the glass, I'd put a cowmint plant down the end of his musket and make John Brown smile for good.

I dashed back across the street to tell Mr. Richmond about our discovery. Daniel answered the door. At sixteen, Jerry's age, he already had whiskers, an Adam's apple, and hairy legs. The first time my mother saw him, she remarked, "My, that boy certainly is mature-looking for his age," which was her way of saying he was too good-looking for his own good. Daniel told me to be quiet. His father was "rehearsing." I could hear Mr. Richmond in the background, his voice loud and strange. When I went into the main room, there were Jerry and Robbie, grinning at me for having beaten me over here. I went on in quietly and sat at the back of the room with them, not on the good chairs, but squatted down with them in my dirty jeans and listened.

Right away the house felt different. It was my brothers on either side of me, and the three of us crouched down like gargoyles, as if too dirty to use the furniture. The other night, when I came over with Mom and Dad, I ended up sitting in any chair I wanted. I had felt at home. Now, with my brothers, I was sitting on the floor like a little monkey. Jerry and Robbie, meanwhile, were glancing around, probably for Ricky Hardaway, expecting him to step out from behind a door like a crazed, bucktoothed hillbilly.

It did not take long to see, in this house of mirrors, how different my brothers and I were from the Richmonds. We were like the weeds out back. Buckthorn, quack grass, and pigweed, mixed in with lamb's quarter, buttonweed, and dog fennel—plants Dad said shouldn't be a thousand miles of one another, but were.

Meanwhile, Mr. Richmond, pacing around in front of the room, was belting out strange phrases—"Is this my unthankful king? He who is dead is next of blood?" Alex stood following along in a small book. Luke sat in a fancy old chair, his legs dunked over the armrest, his pale-blue face wrapped up in his father. Daniel stood, arms crossed, in the doorway. On the frosted glass coffee table in the center of the room lay a thick glossy book with raised gold letters, *The*

Complete Works of William Shakespeare. Beside it was a stack of smaller books. *Othello,* the top one read, in gold letters.

No way in the world my brothers and I could understand Shakespeare. What kid growing up in West Virginia could? In school, we put up with all the "Wherefore art thou's" we had to, but at home, the only book my brothers and I read was *TV Guide.* Mom got us a set of Funk & Wagnalls once to try to change all that, but the whole sixteen books got accidentally recycled.

Suddenly, Mr. Richmond cried out—"Let my soul want mercy, if I shall not join with him!"

When he pretended to cry, making a silly weeping sound, my brothers started grinning—and Jerry even snickered! Luke shot them a mean look, then sat glaring at them. He gave me one or two glances as well.

When Mr. Richmond continued, saying everything backward and with an exclamation point—"Away, I say! How now, but hark!"—Jerry sighed and muttered something. Mr. Richmond stopped and looked up. The whole house stopped and looked up. I felt my body go to stone. I could only wish I were a gargoyle, high up and far away from here.

In that instant, Ricky Hardaway came through the house, dressed in work clothes, carrying two paint cans. He sauntered down the hall and glanced over as he passed. When he saw my brothers and me in the big living room, he stopped and stared.

Mr. Richmond, meanwhile, looking more concerned

than angered by my brother's snide remark, stepped around the white sofa with the curlicue arms, took Alex's small play-book from him, and held it out for Jerry.

"No way," said my idiot brother, leaning back.

I was dead with embarrassment. I always knew this moment would come, but you just don't know how embarrassed you could possibly be until you're with your redneck brothers in a palace of mirrors, listening to Shakespeare, and one of them makes a stupid remark. Whatever my cowmint plant was, it sure wasn't working on Jerry or Robbie.

I looked over at Luke. We were no longer in Grandma's house, gazing downriver together as if looking forever. He was glaring at West Virginia hillbillies in his living room!

Next, Mr. Richmond tried giving the book to Robbie, but he did the same—shook his head in terror.

"No?" Mr. Richmond asked.

My poor brother sat petrified.

"Come on, Robbie," I made the mistake of saying.

"Shut up!" he hissed.

When Mr. Richmond looked at me next, I was waiting, the words on the tip of my tongue—the best new words in my mind since last night.

"I found it. I found cowmint!"

His eyes twinkled, and before I knew it, I was holding the small book. When he explained that Alex and I were playing husband and wife, Jerry let out a loud, snotty laugh. Mr. Richmond, ignoring him, showed me where to start reading.

"Now remember your cue," he said.

Alex cleared his throat. "'Tis very good," he started saying in a fancy-sounding voice like his father's, "I must be circumstanc'd."

"Circumcised?" Jerry howled out, leaning around me and getting Robbie to laugh.

Luke and Alex groaned, and Daniel even told my brother to shut up. Mr. Richmond, ignoring him again, nodded at me to read.

"It is the cause," I read, "it is—"

But I lost my place, and both my brothers laughed again. Mr. Richmond quickly pointed to the spot on the page.

"It is the cause of my soul," he read for me.

Alex, standing nearby, raised his hands and said all dramatically, "It is the cause? I'll not shed my blood!"

Mr. Richmond pointed to my next line, and as if my life depended on it, I kept my eye on his finger.

"Yet she must die . . . ," Mr. Richmond said, getting me started again.

"Yet she must die, else she'll betray more men."

At this point, he told me I was supposed to pretend to take out my sword. So I did.

"It's not a penknife, son," Mr. Richmond said—my gross brothers laughed—"it's a sword!"

He yanked out an invisible sword of his own, as long as a broomstick, and held it high above him, his eyes full of crazy fury. I pulled out my own big imaginary sword, too. It was so big I stumbled holding onto it, and Mr. Richmond smiled.

"I would not kill thy unprepared spirit," I read without one mistake, following his finger. "No. Heaven forfend."

"No!" he shouted. "Heaven forfend!"

Luke leaned out of his chair. "Josh, shout like you did in the cave."

"No!" I shouted. "Heaven forfend!"

I could hear my voice lift into every corner of this big room, but still it wasn't enough. Mr. Richmond lifted his hands, telling me to be even louder. So I flat-out screamed it, my voice fraying like a rag. My stupid brothers were snickering, but Mr. Richmond was nodding me on.

"I would not kill thy unprepared spirit! I must change thy heart to meet the coming day." I took in a deep breath—I could see myself in every single mirror in this room, dozens of me and me alone reflecting and shimmering and smiling back at myself like the king or god I was—and yelled: "Nay, I must change for the coming day!"

I must change for the coming day!

I must change for the coming day!

I must change for the coming day!

My voice lifted up into a great echo, going up and around, up and around, into every fancy room in this house. Stars were shooting across my eyes from the dizziness, and Jerry and Robbie were gaping at me as if I'd be sick in the hospital for weeks for exerting myself so. Behind them, all the gold and silver things in this house were twinkling, like on Christmas when you step up to the decorated tree and peer into the prettiest ball of all.

Mr. Richmond took a big step back, bowed, and said, smiling down at me, "Good." He looked a moment longer. "Very good."

All around me, Daniel, Alex, and Luke were clapping. I even saw Ricky Hardaway smiling at me from the far corner of the room. Sparkles blurred in my eyes, and a big smile hung on my face. I wanted to tell my mother, and I especially wanted to tell my father. It *was* the power of cowmint!

CHAPTER X: THE LONELY PIG PATH

IT WOULD BE THE BEGINNING of a big change in my life. Day after day I ran next door to the Richmonds' and stayed as long as I could. Sometimes my brothers came along, but I was happier when they didn't. The Richmonds' house was a place of great fun, sometimes crazy fun. The top two floors were still being worked on, but other than that, the place was wide open. Mr. Richmond had a ton of playbooks from when he had taught acting in Boston, before he became a historian. Alex, Luke, and I, sometimes Daniel, too, read from *Cat on a Hot Tin Roof* and *Death of a Salesman*. Mr. Richmond also had a big box of old stage costumes. We put on pirate patches, cowboy hats, jester masks, even Cleopatra and Elvis Presley wigs, then ran around the house, acting nutty. There was a piano on the second floor that Alex could play pretty well, everything from Scott Joplin's "Solace" to the "Jelly Roll Blues." There was a freedom to their house that made me totally happy. No longer was my life slow and brown, like the ugly Potomac River. As I ran down the pig path between our houses, I had the feeling I was running along the wishbone of the rivers, taking the luckier, faster, greener Shenandoah to my future. Along the path were my cowmint plants, glistening green and blue in the sunlight, the long stems bending toward me as I passed, as if to sprinkle more magic dust on me.

Since I was so good in the *Othello* read-through, Mr. Richmond invited me to be in the big John Brown play this summer—get this—to play one of John Brown's sons. Luke and Alex were playing Oliver and Owen Brown, and I was to be Frederick Brown. My line was the best, too: "I stand here today, before God and country, in defense of my father, for his actions are brave and of the noblest!" I would even get to raise my arm like a sword.

I couldn't believe it—me playing John Brown's son in a fancy house in the richest part of town? Mr. Richmond my "father"? It was as if I had pulled on the wishbone of the rivers and won! Wish granted.

For my brothers, it was a far different story. They started out taking small roles, but still couldn't fit in at all. All they did was cause trouble. If they weren't snickering at everything the Richmonds did, they were pushing them around, acting like bullies. The clincher for Mr. Richmond was when Jerry started shoving Daniel around in the hallway, nearly tipping over one of the gigantic vases.

"Jerry, if you can't behave yourself, you're not welcome over here!" Mr. Richmond shouted.

It was the first time I saw Mr. Richmond lose his temper. He could be John Brown after all. You could hear the thunder come down in his voice and see the rain pour all over Jerry. It would be the last time Jerry set foot at the Richmonds'. Robbie, too.

Days later, Daniel asked me, "Why are your brothers that way?"

Luke's eyes came in clear behind his glasses. He wanted to know, too. So did Alex. As the three of them stood looking at me, suddenly, the distance between our houses no longer seemed to be twenty or thirty yards across the vacant lot, but twenty or thirty miles, and, somehow, in the strangest way, twenty or thirty years.

I knew how my brothers seemed to them. It was like Jerry and Robbie wanted bad things to happen to themselves and did everything to make sure they did. They were like scared horses running right into the fire.

If there was one difference between my brothers and me, it was that I knew how to act like Mom at the right moments—when to keep my mouth shut and when to copy the Richmonds, laughing whenever they did, looking serious at the right times.

While my days were filled with Shakespeare and John Brown, my father went back to his old miserable self. It was like cowmint never happened. He started working long hours at the post office. His mail route had been expanded, our mother told us, which meant he was at war with the postmaster again. He came home all the more tired and grouchy. Long gone from his face was that weird smile I had seen that evening when he tried to take my drawing pencil and sketchpad from me, while my cowmint lay on the table before us like a miracle plant. Longer gone was that moment on the third floor of the Richmonds' house, at the end of the hall, by the window overlooking the weedy lot, when he told Mr. Richmond the cowmint story. I didn't dare ask him if the expert on his mail route had identified the plant yet. I didn't want to know. From the look on his face, there was no way the answer could be good.

When he found out about Jerry's little run-in with Mr. Richmond and that my brothers were no longer welcome next door, he was so angry he wanted to put a stop to all of us visiting next door, including me.

"Katie, if we let these damn kids have their way," he said, pointing around the kitchen table at each of us, "it won't be a week before one of them's throwin' a rock through a window over there, or tracking dirt into their house, or bothering them somehow."

"Well, Bill," Mom said, sitting stiffly between my father and me as always, "I'm sure your son is no bother."

Jerry and Robbie looked up. Dad lowered his spoon.

"Which son, Katie? I have three," he said.

Mom said nothing, just kept her face buried in her food.

"Katie, I'm waiting."

"Yeah, why's he get to go over?" Jerry blurted out, pointing at me.

"Bill, if Luke's invited Josh over and it's all right with Niles—"

"And what about your other two *sons*, Katie?" He pointed his finger across the table at me, dragging his sleeve across her plate and mine. "You've always favored that damn boy of yours."

"Yeah!"

"Shut up, Jerry!" he barked.

Mom slammed her fork down on the table.

"Then *what* are any of these boys going to do with their summer, Bill? You won't allow them to go anywhere as it is."

"Go anywhere?" he said, his face getting redder. "Where in the hell are they going to go and not get into trouble?"

Robbie shot his snotty voice across the table. "The Richmonds get to go anywhere they want."

"That, mister," Dad said, leveling his finger at my brother, "is because they know how to behave. You all don't."

"Oh, Bill, do you know what you're saying?"

"Yes, I do, Katie. I do!"

He rapped his chest several times with his fist to show that he was still head of this family—rapped it so hard his voice rattled like weights in a grandfather clock. Whatever my plant was, it sure wasn't curing him. He was angrier than ever. Maybe he did need confession after all.

As June turned to July, the Richmonds' house became my getaway. Every morning I ran next door before anyone could stop me—before Jerry could shoot his BB gun at me, before Robbie could wing a rotten apple at me, before Dad could growl to Mom that I should be spending time more usefully, although he never had an answer as to how.

Mr. Richmond was never unhappy to find me on his doorstep with the morning paper.

"Well, here's the next John Brown!" he would roar playfully.

He always smiled at me, invited me in, and fixed me toast along with everyone else. It was during these moments, around the kitchen table, that I wondered about the Richmonds' mother—who she was, why she wasn't here with them, whether they ever missed her. They never spoke about her, and I never felt right just asking about her. Still, they seemed twice as strong inside without her. It made me wonder how this could be. Why, when they had only one parent instead of two, were they twice as grown up as my brothers and me? All I could think was that, whoever their mother was, she must be the saddest woman on earth for not being with this cool family.

I wondered about the Richmonds' house, too. One morning, when Mr. Richmond sent me upstairs for a play-book, I found a rope across the doorway to one of the fancy rooms, just like in a museum. I stopped and drew my hand across the long, velvety red rope. I never even told Luke I saw the strange rope.

Another day, when I ran upstairs for something else, I found a big closet that was completely empty. Nothing inside it but a burning light bulb and a clothes hanger.

It was like the Richmonds had never completely moved in.

Whenever I could, I peeked up the stairs to the fourth floor, waiting for the day when the top part of the house would be finished. But always there were paint cans stacked on the steps, turning me back.

Since Mr. Richmond worked just down the hill at the park offices, he came home for lunch and sometimes rehearsed for the John Brown play with a takeout sub in his hand. He paced around the big living room, glancing down at his playbook before roaring out his lines to the ceiling and raising his sandwich overhead like a sword. Sitting on the sofa with Luke, I loved watching his father become angry whenever he wanted, belting out, "For I have not forsaken man large or small!" Then, seconds later, he'd smile at us as if nothing had happened. Mr. Richmond could turn anger off and on like a switch!

One of the best things about the Richmonds' house was that it was never empty of people. There were park people always coming over, lots of park people—the skinny lady who ran the bookstore, the pretty girl who worked in the Visitor's Center, and important men dressed in suits. Even park rangers came into the Richmonds' house. In their fancy forest-green uniforms, they stood smiling around at Mr. Richmond's nice furniture. Then they went into the big kitchen with Mr. Richmond, chatting, their wide-brim hats in their hands. When they saw me with Luke, they didn't frown at me or even recognize me as a Connors boy from next door. If I was a friend of the Richmonds', then I was okay in their book, too.

Even Father Ron stopped by one afternoon. He wasn't wearing his stiff white priest's collar as usual, but a flannel shirt and blue jeans with rolled-up cuffs. I couldn't believe it—he wasn't dressed much better than me!

Mr. Richmond, turning me by my shoulders toward Father Ron's soft face smiling down, said, "Ronald, meet the young discoverer of cowmint."

"*Cowmen,* did you say?"

"No, heaven forfend!" shouted Mr. Richmond. "Cow-*mint!*"

His loud, playful voice made Father Ron and me smile.

"It heals the heart of ignorance," Mr. Richmond said.

"Heals the heart of ignorance?" Father Ron said, with a grin. "Well, that's some plant. And you discovered it?"

I nodded as hard as I could.

"You know, Niles," he said, turning to Mr. Richmond, "I wonder if we have 'cow-mint' growing in our church garden." Father Ron turned back to me. "Hey, I have an idea. You can be the church's official cowmint expert, okay? Maybe someday you'll come and take a look, as the official expert, okay, Josh?"

As I grinned and nodded, I found myself liking him. He was tall like my father, rocked on his heels like my father, and wore an old-fashioned metal watchband like my father. He had the same short hair and even a mole on his cheek. He didn't look "liberal" to me. He wasn't wearing an earring or walking around with a pierced tongue. Upon closer look, he didn't resemble at all the priest in the old picture we had. Mom was right. I was just seeing the cleric's collar. I couldn't imagine who in the world my father thought Father Ron was like.

As I spent more and more time at the Richmonds', I began to realize that none of Mr. Richmond's important visitors ever minded me being there with them. One time I was standing right beside Lee Jackson, the richest man in town, and didn't feel bad. It was like he didn't even recognize me, when I knew he did. It was like on Halloween when, wearing my Casper the Friendly Ghost mask, I could knock on any door in town and not feel ashamed of who I was. I was so far off King Kong's island it wasn't funny!

But always I had to go back home. I felt I was in a fairy tale, escaping to a magical castle by day, returning to an ogre's shack at night. When I raised my eyes from the dirt path, I saw my horrible little house waiting for me—the heaps of rusted junk, the rotting trees, the moldy stone side of our house. Inside my house, I saw every crack in our yucky yellow walls, every scuff mark around our icky green baseboards, every worn-out piece of furniture. There was my poor mother, putting Lemon Pledge on her pieces of junk. She made me want to cry.

Soon I couldn't stand looking at anything in my house anymore—not the chipped-up plates I had been eating off all my life, not the forks gnawed on a million times, not our old refrigerator rusted around the handle. I couldn't stand looking at my jerk brothers, either, lying around and eating junk food, watching TV, playing video games, doing nothing with their summer, prisoners on Dad's island of junk and trees.

My father was the hardest to be around. Evening after evening, I waited with dread for him to come home from the mail route and tell me that my cowmint plant was nothing but eastern chokeweed or flowered bent grass, some plant in his books he had overlooked. I was worried he'd try to take back the magic my plant had put into my life, that he'd make my life how it was before. I got in the habit, before dinner, of glancing around his side of the living room, expecting to find my plant lying on top of his latest *Popular Mechanics*, freeze-dried inside a plastic Baggie, labeled some crazy name like Mouse-Ear Chickweed or Pineapple Pigweed. During dinner, I waited for him to toss the Baggie into the center of the table and say to me, "Okay, smartie, I told you so." So I kept my eyes buried in the white hills of my mashed potatoes.

One evening he pushed his plate aside and sat glaring at the thick wall between us and the church.

"That damn house over there, Katie—it's causing me nothing but trouble." He turned to her. "Lee Jackson double-parking his damn Mercedes in front of my house whenever he pleases, just to go next door—you know that SOB just wants to buy my property so that he can put up another of his tacky souvenir shops."

He glowered around the room, looking for something to disapprove of.

"Oh, something else. I almost forgot."

He slapped his hand down on the table, snapping Jerry and Robbie out of their comalike gazes at their salmon cakes.

"Let me tell you all something about your damn cousin Ricky," he said, pointing his fork at each of us. "Katie, you listen, too. You'll think twice now about ever letting him get close to this house."

He squared his chair with the table and started tapping the end of his fork against his plate.

"Gus Jenkins, out by the underpass, saw someone just last week who looked like Ricky Hardaway paddling over to your all grandmother's old house"—he pointed the fork around the table at each of us—"from the Maryland side of the river."

Jerry's eyes went wide.

"Paddling?" Mom said.

"Yes, with what sounded like a damn bell in the middle of his canoe," Dad said.

"A bell?"

"Yes, a bell. Now listen—"

"The chapel bell!" Jerry blurted out. "You mean Ricky stole it?"

Dad was quick to nod. But Mom, looking around, was confused. So was I.

"Bill, that bell's been gone for years," she said.

"Katie, I'm just telling you what I was told," he said, throwing his hands up.

He turned his chair away from the table.

"Whatever, that damn boy has no business being around that old house. No business. Goofy little bastard probably broke the arms off that statue out there, too." He took out his pipe and started smacking the bowl of it against his palm. "As if that place hasn't been picked clean already." He stood and looked for matches on the pie safe. "No, sir, I've changed my mind about that damn Niles. And I tried to warn him about Ricky."

He went on muttering about all the traffic going in and out next door, car doors slamming, music playing.

"Hey, speak of the devil," Robbie called out from the window.

Jerry was the first to hop up from the table and rush to the window. I was right behind him, half expecting to see Mr. Richmond or Father Ron. But down in the street was Ricky, giving a tourist directions. As he pointed this way, then that, Mom, peering over our shoulders, started groaning and snickering, as if she couldn't make up her mind whether it was sad or funny, Ricky Hardaway talking to a tourist. I was grinning along with her. All of us, including Dad, watched through the blinds as Ricky moved over by the rock wall in front of our house and started talking to another tourist—a girl. That was something to see—Ricky in his dirty tank top, tattoos showing, talking to a pretty girl. Jerry and Robbie were breathing all over the glass, amazed. Dad's eye was against the blind as if peering down the barrel of one of his rifles. First time the five of us ever did anything together, and it was spying on Ricky.

"I can certainly see why Niles likes him," Mom said.

"Niles," said my father bitterly.

"Yes, Bill, Niles," she said, turning from the window. "Look at the good job he's done for Niles."

"Father Ron recommended him," I said, from a safe distance.

Dad whirled around.

"How in the hell you know that?" he snapped.

"He did, Josh?" my mother asked.

When I nodded, she turned to Dad.

"Bill?"

123

She was standing between Dad and me, and she couldn't hide her surprise.

"Oh, Katie, don't look so damn impressed," he growled. "The goofy boy scratches around in the church flower bed for that flaky Father 'Ron,' doing some kind of crazy landscaping work."

Jerry's big mouth blared out: "Ricky does work for the church?"

Dad went on to insult both of them, especially Ricky, whom he wouldn't hire, he said, to roll a flat tire up to a filling station.

"Katie," he said, going back to the table and slamming his hand back down on it again, rattling plates, "I'm thinking of putting up a damn fence."

"A fence?" she cried out. "Oh, good lord, Bill, no."

"Yes, a fence. Around the whole place. It's the only answer."

She went over to the stove and started banging pots around.

"Then I wanna move, Bill," she said, her back to him. "I'm putting my foot down, too!"

He popped out a laugh. Jerry and Robbie looked scared to death. I wasn't. I was amazed. My mother putting her foot down?

"Move?" He looked at her. "Move where?"

But she didn't have an answer, because there was no answer. The moment stopped like the tip of Mount Everest. There was just nowhere for us to go.

CHAPTER XI: THE SOUND OF THE CHURCH BELLS

J ERRY, DURING THIS TIME IN July, was doing his best to torture me. An outcast from the Richmonds', he had nothing to lose. He stuck nettles in my bed—dirt, roots, and all.

"Look, it's cowmint! It's cowmint!" he cried out like an idiot from the bottom bunk, kicking my mattress up and sending dirt and roots all over the room.

Over and over he gave my mattress a swift kick, sending my face within inches of our plaster of Paris ceiling. The jerk loved to jab his heels into my mattress and bounce me around like a ball on the nose of a seal.

Then he pointed one of my colored pencils overhead like a sword, all but jabbing it into my mattress.

"Nay, heaven *fart*-fend!"

He had Robbie doubled over with laughter.

Egghead, snot, corncob teeth—I got called them all. When I cleaned up the nettles, he just stuffed crabgrass into my shirt pockets. When I cleaned that up, I found maple leaves in my juice glass. Mom told me to do my best to ignore him. My brother was on a belligerent course, she said, and we all knew why.

He was burning up with jealousy for Daniel. Though in town for only little more than a month, sissy rich-boy Daniel was already seeing some girl who worked for the park. He even got to take her all the way to Ocean City one weekend in his father's Toyota. All my brother ever got to drive was Uncle Dave's tractor. Already Daniel had everything—car, girl, and freedom.

All this unfairness in the world left Jerry in front of our tiny bathroom mirror, seeing what little he had. Why did he have to have a crew cut every month? Why did his hair, what little he had, have to be red like Mom's? Why did he have to have freckles? Why no cell phone? *Why, why, why?* On top of that, that no-good Ricky Hardaway, he complained, got paid to work for the church!

His only happiness was to pick on Robbie and me. With Robbie, his latest put-down was that he and I were "butt buddies," a remark that always led to the two of them fighting on the floor, shaking the whole house, and breaking something.

Robbie, during this time, wasn't saying much, though I did catch him once with black dirt on his jeans. Very black dirt: coal. There was only one place on this end of Jefferson County where someone could get coal stains on their cuffs—River Road. It ran up the Potomac, between the train tracks and the bank, to the lane that led up to the white house. It worried me to think of my strange brother sneaking out there by himself. That house was like a maze no one should get lost in.

All in all, I was always glad to get away from my crazy family and go next door. Sometimes on my way over to the Richmonds', I would stop in my cowmint patch with my sketchpad and colored pencils. Mr. Richmond, it seemed, liked my patch, too.

"Beautiful plants," he said one day, stepping through the weeds between our houses to find me there.

I watched him turn and gaze across the lot at what he could see of my little house tucked back under the trees. Funny, my father had the same arms-folded stance from the side door whenever he stared in this direction.

"Your father sure likes his privacy," Mr. Richmond said. "I admire him for not selling."

"A man's home is a man's home," I said.

He turned to me. "He said that?"

I nodded.

"Well, that I understand," he said, his voice trailing away.

As I looked up at him, I could see sadness on his face. Maybe from my father not visiting him anymore. Maybe that hurt his feelings, and he wondered why Dad was staying away.

My eyes followed the blue and white zebra stripes in his shirt down to his belt. He wasn't wearing his park uniform, so he looked like a plain person. His khaki slacks were okay, but his shoes—I couldn't believe it—were cheap Payless loafers, the kind with glued-on spongy yellow soles. Jerry once had the same kind in his size, and when the soles started peeling off shortly after he began wearing them, Mom returned them.

Mr. Richmond stood looking down at my cowmint plants. To make the seven plants all the more special, I had placed a ring of white stones around them, along with the prettiest purple and red rocks I could find. Mr. Richmond, noticing this, had a smile on his face. But I knew he'd smile at prickly greenbrier decorated the same way.

"By the way, did your father ever get it identified?" he asked, nodding down at the plants.

I shook my head.

"Not yet," I said.

"Well, it almost doesn't matter what it really is, does it?" he said, looking down at the plants. "As long as you believe in it."

But I could tell he didn't really believe what he said. If my father was miserable for the rest of his life, somehow he'd make me miserable, too, so it mattered.

LATE ONE AFTERNOON, after Luke and I had run all over town, we were tending to the cowmint patch, weeding and watering it, when a dark figure moved in the corner of my eye.

My father!

"What are *you* doing over here?" he asked Luke first.

If his harsh voice wasn't enough, one look at his face, and I could see he was still on the outs with life.

He spotted Mom's good watering can in my hand, and, from there, his eyes moved along the ground to my cowmint patch. Looking at the ring of pretty white stones around my plants, he got a kink in his face, a twisted-up, embarrassed smile. I knew what he was thinking. *I was a kooky kid.* I didn't like tools or working on cars. I preferred silly nonsense like this.

When he turned and looked at me with his strict face, I could feel the end closing in.

"Luke, shouldn't you be home by now?" he said.

Luke, looking scared, took off running, leaving me to my father.

"Josh," he said, glad to take a few steps away from me, where he stood and looked off into nowhere, "I don't know how in the hell these crazy ideas get into your foolish head."

I watched his eyes drift off to the left, in the direction of the Richmonds' big white house.

"The hell I don't," he growled.

When he took a step back and stumbled over a clump of dirt in the torn-up lot, an angry look came over his face.

"Look at this damn place," he growled. "You just had to kick over every damn plant out here, didn't you?" He turned to me, his face getting redder. "Some of these plants were rare. Special."

Special! I couldn't believe him. My cowmint was special! Why didn't he believe that?

"And another thing," he said, pointing his ugly finger at me, "before I forget." He looked at me for a second until he was sure he had my attention. "You're not to be in that damn John Brown play!"

I stood straight up. How'd he know? *Jerry, that rat!*

"No matter what Niles Richmond says, I forbid you, you hear me?" he said.

He came closer, all but jabbing his finger into my chest.

"Buster, if you're in that play, don't even bother coming home!"

"Why?" I shouted out, backing up and tripping over a clump of dirt myself.

"None of your business *why*. Just do as you're told, you hear me?"

He pointed down at the mess of weeds and dirt I had just stumbled over.

"These poor plants went undisturbed for fifty years until you came along stomping all over them." He started toward me, ready to give me a good kick in the rump. "Boy, you've caused me a lot of grief—"

Suddenly, from above came the loudest church bells, banging and clanging as if the massive steeple of St. Peter's next door was finally falling on our rotten little house. It was Wednesday, and the church always made a special racket with the bells on Wednesday. As my father looked up through the patchy tent of trees over our yard, scowling at the racket, I hightailed it out of sight. His awful words couldn't hurt me if I wasn't around to hear them!

I ran around the junk piles in our yard, up the rickety back porch, and into our dingy kitchen.

"Mom!" I cried out, coming to a stop and standing there, the tears starting.

She figured out from my wrenched-up face what had

just happened. She stood up from the table and came over to me just as I started crying.

"Oh, Josh, you didn't do anything wrong," she said, putting her arms around me. "Maybe you got just a little carried away with that whole plant business."

I looked up at her.

"But so did you," I said. "You said I'd know when I saw it!"

She looked away.

"Yes, I know I did. Niles Richmond is—well, his enthusiasm over that plant was very *persuasive.* I can certainly see why you kids like him so."

With her arm loosely around me, I stood looking down at the grimy tile floor of our kitchen.

"Dad hates me," I said.

"Oh, Josh, he doesn't hate you."

"Then why can't I be in the John Brown play?"

She took her arm away.

"Oh," she said, her voice becoming chilly as she took a step away from me. "So that's what this is about?" I watched as she began a long, slow walk around the kitchen table. "Josh, I'm afraid *that* is out of the question. Don't even consider it. Get the idea out of your head right now." She turned and looked at me for a moment. "Please. You *must, must* not be in that play."

I stood looking at her. What in the world was she so freaked out about? It was just a stupid play. So what if it was in some big fancy house? I wasn't scared.

"Mr. Richmond said I could," I said.

"Yes, I'm sure he did," she said, walking on around the table. "But your father and I say you can't, so I'm afraid you'll just have to listen to us."

I stood there. It was almost as if she was scared—so scared of something I could see bones pushing around in her forehead.

"Josh," she went on to say, rubbing her hands, which she did sometimes for her arthritis, "they're just not our type of people up there."

"Nobody's our type of people," I muttered.

"Now watch your mouth, young man."

I stood sulking, then glaring, whichever worked best from second to second.

"Besides," she said, "there's a certain person in particular in that play every year—good lord, I shouldn't even be telling you this—that your father simply does not approve of."

Who was she kidding? In a room of ten people, my father could find a hundred people he simply did not approve of. I zeroed in on her.

"Who?" I asked.

She laughed out loud and took a step back.

"Well, I'm not gonna to tell you that, good heavens," she said, giving me her "you're ridiculous" grin. "You should know better than to even ask."

When she started pretending to straighten up the *Family Circle* magazines on the table, as if putting an end to the conversation, I went back to sulking.

"Dad's just jealous of Mr. Richmond," I said.

"Oh, good lord," she said, turning to me and crossing her arms, "now where'd you hear that? Your brother?"

I knew my mother would never admit it, but the world could see that Mr. Richmond was the better father. He had done everything right with Daniel, Alex, and Luke, and Dad had done everything wrong with us. It was as a simple as that.

When I didn't look sorry for what I had said, Mom stood looking away, shaking her head, her hand on the table as if needing it to hold herself up.

"Yes, Josh, your father and I have always been at odds on how to raise you all. Especially you. And I'm afraid I've shown *you* favoritism, as he just loves to remind me."

I sighed as loud as I could. This I had heard all before. I had no pity for her when she tried to back out of having been nice to me. Alex and Luke were nice to each other every day, and they never had to regret it.

"Mom, you were the one who said he needed to go to confession!" I said, raising my voice.

She turned to me so fast it was almost cruel how startled she was.

There. It was out in the open. Now she'd have to explain. I watched and waited. But a horrible look came over her face.

"Who told you that?" she burst out. "And you've got one second to tell me, young man!"

"I was outside, Mom!"

I pointed to the stupid window where I had listened in, and she looked at me for a moment until finally believing me. Then she said in her coldest voice, "Josh, whatever you overheard, you got your information wrong."

She reached down and picked a speck of something off the floor.

"Or not entirely right."

I waited for her to say more. But she didn't. She calmly sat, opened one of her stupid women's magazines, and pretended to read.

I turned, stepped out into the living room, and stood below the big bookcase holding the high shelf of family photo albums.

"Mom," I said, my voice coolly crossing the room to her, "what happened to that old picture we had of the priest on Grandma's porch?"

I stood facing the bookcase, my head turned to her, daring her to answer.

"It's not in the photo album anymore," I said.

But she was like a radio turned off. She even shifted her chair a little and sat with her back to me, the way our house stood with its back to the church.

I definitely knew something. Just what it was, I didn't yet know.

CHAPTER XII: THE MYSTERY OF THE ROPED-OFF ROOMS

THE RICHMONDS' HOUSE, during this time, was becoming a little strange to me. Not only were two more rooms roped off, but the kitchen didn't make sense. As new and shiny as it was, it had way less food in it than it should have. In one whole big cupboard there was just one box of Cheerios, and it was the small kind.

I knew that the Richmonds didn't have a mother around and that they ordered in a lot and probably needed to go to the grocery store, but it was ridiculous how much more food we had in our ugly little house. Our freezer was packed with hot dogs and ice cream, and our refrigerator was so full you couldn't see shelves. Dad often thought the light was out because something was always jammed up against it.

One day, when I went into the Richmonds' fancy high-ceilinged bathroom, I couldn't find any toilet paper. The soap dish was empty as well. I peeked into the shower—shampoo bottles were low. I even opened the medicine cabinet. No Band-Aids? What did they do when they cut themselves?

Not many days later, while I was looking for Luke and I peered up the stairs to the fourth floor, I saw that the paint cans that had been blocking the steps were now gone. The house was finished!

Eagerly, I went up. But step after step, I couldn't believe what I was seeing. Everything was smaller up here, the rooms and windows. The ceilings were lower, too. More than that, there was nothing much up here, except paint cans and drop cloths. In one room was just a chair. In another, a telephone book and a lamp without a shade. The walls were freshly painted white, but blank, no pictures, no furniture, just vacant rooms, a barren hallway, and a sanded hardwood floor without its glossy yellow gleam. It was like the Richmonds' house was one big watercolor, but the artist didn't finish.

I stopped, stood, and listened. Nothing but eerie silence and the strangeness of seeing an end to the Richmonds' nice things. A haunting feeling came over me. I felt the same emptiness I had always felt in Grandma's house up the river. In that second, I wanted to run and tell my father about this floor. Not Mom, just Dad. I wanted to tell my father with the same urgency as if someone were robbing the Richmonds blind, leaving their house empty, just as someone had left Grandma's.

Cautious step after cautious step, I went on exploring. In one room was something that made me stop and stare: a brand-new box spring and mattress, both still in plastic, stacked up one-two in the middle of the floor, as if delivered ahead of time, the rest of the room waiting to be furnished around it. As I stood looking at the embroidered blue swirls in the mattress's surface, I thought of the dirty little half-size prison-striped mattress in my father's childhood room. Looking at this one made that one all the more harsh and lonely.

Then I did something really weird. After checking around to make sure I was alone, I climbed up on this big plastic-covered mattress, stretched out on my back, and started flapping my arms and legs, as if making a snow angel. I was totally silly, grinning my head off, the heavy plastic crinkling under me. One thing I could never tell Luke, or anybody, was that once when I sneaked out to Grandma's house, I actually lay down on that filthy little mattress out there to see how it felt. It was hard and awful, and in seconds I jumped up and ran out of the house. I wondered why, in that whole big house up the river, my father had ended up in the smallest room on the top floor. Not that I could ever ask him. But if he wasn't so mean and ugly, I'd say my father was like Rapunzel needing to be rescued from the castle tower.

I hopped off this spanking new mattress and stood looking at it again, grinning and shaking my head at how strange I was.

Another room on the fourth floor, though empty of furniture, had long white curtains. I pushed them out the windows and let them wrap around the side of the house in the breeze, making a woman's long hair out of them. I had never been so high over the town. I could see tourists on the hill, the roofs of all the shops, the rivers. When I looked straight down, I saw our house—the big rust stain on our roof, the white plastic sewer pipes, the dirt yard and pig paths my brothers and I had worn through the trees, trying to find ways to leave the house without being seen by tourists. I saw my poor mother in the kitchen, too, through the little window half covered with insulation. As I stood looking down at her far below, she looked like a tiny woman trapped in an old dollhouse.

Served her right. I was tired of her cringing around Dad. *Certain person in that play.* Who was she kidding? My father disapproved of half the town. *I'm not prepared to discuss that with you.* Fine.

The longer I looked out, the more it seemed I was seeing my life from a different angle, as if outside my body. It made me think that for as long as I had been living in this town, I had seen only a tiny part of it. I imagined myself becoming a rich artist and buying this house one day and living here for the rest of my life, and always I would look out this window, knowing I hadn't stayed in that little house next door.

Then my eyes caught sight of someone down in the street staring up at me.

Ricky Hardaway!

I reeled back from the window, only to inch close to it again. No, wait. It wasn't Ricky, but someone who looked just like him—same long blond hair, same scruffy look. While I peered down, trying to make out his face, this person was peering up, trying to do the same with mine. It was a strange moment while the two of us were hooked in a stare at each other, neither knowing who the other was.

Then I recognized the face.

Snake Wilson!

I jumped back from the window. Snake Wilson was nobody to stare at. He really did run over his stepfather with a lawn tractor.

As I kept backing away from the window, I heard a voice behind me that sent me through the ceiling.

"Hey, cous."

I spun around.

Ricky!

He was stepping out from behind a door, grinning, holding a paintbrush. I stood gasping for air.

"Sorry, bud," he said.

I could see he had been painting, as his hair, face, and arms were spotted with fresh white paint. But why was he being sneaky about it? I worried that he and Snake Wilson were up to something, and I might have to run for my life. I especially thought so when he stepped past me to the window as if to signal Snake to come up and help him kill me. They'd probably dissolve me inside a paint can, then brush me all over the walls so that no one would ever find me.

I felt trapped in the castle tower while Ricky stood staring down at the street. I waited for him to turn mean, Snake Wilson somehow telling him to. But he said nothing, just kept staring down. Slowly, I eased over to the window beside him.

Snake Wilson was gone!

"Man, your old man sure is a hoarder," Ricky said, turning and looking out the other side of the window at my house.

From this high up, we could see the rolls of roofing paper and old bricks Dad had us stack up in the yard because they might be worth something someday. We could see the old gutters, the water pipe left aboveground and covered with heat tape, the screen door falling off the back door. I expected Ricky to say it was all gross. I expected him to say our house was falling down. But he didn't.

"Man, your place just needs some work," he said, as if he could do all the work himself in an afternoon.

It was the strangest feeling, standing above the town with my bad cousin, both of us looking at the junky house my father thought he had hidden. It was like having someone know the worst part of you and you feeling better for it.

Then I saw Ricky look across the roof of my house at the big church steeple that stepped down into the crannies of our little town, trying not to knock over houses as easily as bottles and shoe boxes.

"You like Father Ron?" I asked, my nose wrinkled up.

Ricky's dead eye locked on me for a long second.

"Hell, yeah," he said. "He's cool."

I looked down at the floor.

"Dad doesn't," I said.

"Bill?"

I looked up at him again. Did he expect me to call my father by his first name?

"Yeah, well," he said, scratching his whiskered neck with paint-gunked fingernails, "old Bill's a strict son of a bit—"

He caught himself, but I couldn't help but laugh. My father *was* a strict SOB, and we both knew it. He stood grinning at me, and I stood grinning at him. Then he reached for his Coke can on the windowsill.

"Oh, hey," he said. "You find it yet? Your miracle plant?"

I shrugged, half smiled, bunched up my face, did something to answer.

"'Cause I could still use some, cous," he said.

As he stood grinning at me, I knew at that moment he really was my cousin. It was in his horrible smile, all strained up with ugly kindness like a grandmother with arthritis. Even more than that, he put a feeling inside me that he liked me, and a person who likes you, even one as rough as Ricky Hardaway, would never hurt you.

Then I caught myself. What was I doing? I was hanging out with Ricky Hardaway, being chummy-chummy? He was a criminal, Dad always said, and Snake Wilson hanging out down in the street, looking for him, proved it. Quickly, I mumbled something about having to leave, then made my escape downstairs.

JUST DAYS LATER, the fifth floor was finished and waiting for me to explore, too. The steps up were crooked and not covered in fancy red carpet. The walls were bare, too. No mirrors or paintings. Even the banisters looked rickety. I could smell fresh paint and see dust from where the walls had been scraped. As soon as I reached the top step, a voice spoke behind me.

"Hey."

I whirled to see Luke at a window with a pair of binoculars, grinning.

"Guess what? You can see it from here," he said.

I stepped over beside him.

"See what?"

Out the window was a view all way up the Potomac, past the speedboats above the dam, to the bend in the river. With this tall house standing all the taller on the hill, it was like a view from an airplane. You could see the valley furrowing through the mountains, the dark green water lying in its wake in groovy wiggles, like a beautiful mud puddle.

All of a sudden, I got it. I was looking up the river toward Grandma's house, and I could see forever, too! I turned to Luke, my eyes going wide, my mouth falling open.

"You can see my grandma's house from up here?" I said.

Grinning and nodding, he handed me the binoculars, and I found myself peering into the most distant view, my eyes straining as I turned the focus knob, zeroing in on a white speck in the distance.

Grandma's house!

I squinted, blinked, and turned the knob in and out to make sure it wasn't a white rock in the river or a reflection on the water. But there it was! It rose up in the distance with that famous castlelike shape.

My heart was pounding. How was this possible? Did this house grow an extra floor? Did the world get smaller? I wanted to shout out of the window for the whole town to hear—you can see the white house from the top floor of this house!

"Wow!" I cried out.

For a long, wonderful moment, I stood looking through

the binoculars, wishing I could focus in closer and closer, like a high-powered Mars telescope, zoom right in to the top window of Grandma's house and catch someone standing in my father's room by the bum's mattress, looking back downriver at me.

Then, by chance, I scanned the coal-covered River Road that, snaking between the railroad tracks and the riverbank, led up to the white house. Suddenly, I spotted a figure up past the dam, in a bright-white T-shirt. He was walking on the widest, blackest stretch of the road—heading straight for the lane up to the house!

"Hey, someone's going out there!"

Luke leaned over and tried to see through the binoculars at the same time as me.

"Who? Who?" he kept asking. "Lemme see."

I turned the focus knob this way and that way, blurring the tiny figure in, then out. But whoever he was, he was just too far away to make out. All I could see was a white T-shirt and blue jeans. He could be anybody!

Luke grabbed the binoculars and tried to see for himself. He fussed with the knob, then looked for any other knob to turn, to see farther. But no luck.

"Hey, I bet it's your father!" he said, looking over at me, all wide-eyed.

"Nah," I said, trying to laugh about it.

"Your brother then!"

"Stop, jerk."

I snatched the binoculars back and stood spying as best I could on this white-shirted person flickering through the trees, making his way up the leafy lane toward my grandma's old house. Every step he took, I found myself getting angrier and angrier. It was like he was trespassing or something.

I wondered to myself if it was Ricky heading up to the house to smoke dope on the top floor. I thought about what my father had said about Ricky stealing the chapel bell.

"Hey, let's go sneak up on him!" Luke cried out.

He started to dash out of the room, then stopped when he saw me just standing there.

"Come on!" he said.

"Nah."

"Why not?" he cried out. "We can find out who it is."

I wasn't sure why not. Suddenly, I wanted nothing to do with the house. I wanted to be a million miles away from it. Somehow it was ruined now. Who knew how many people sneaked out there? Maybe there were a dozen bums living in it. I wouldn't even have been sad if John Brown had come to life just to burn the house down, like another Missouri farm. He would have, too. It was a worthless, empty house.

Besides, I had this house now, and even with its roped-off rooms and empty closets, this house was way better. With all its high windows, it was like a crystal prism to keep in the palm of my hand. It split up my life, organized it, like light passing through a wedge of glass and coming out yellow, orange, red, blue—all the colors in the rainbow. Out one window I could see our little second-rate house from a bird's-eye view. Out this window, my grandmother's place, itty-bitty in the distance. Out another, the wishbone rivers that the mountains drew back from like stage curtains. Up here I could see in many directions at once, keeping tabs on the world and somehow having a better life at the same time.

But more than anything, in two days I would be playing John Brown's son in the big annual play! No matter what my father wanted.

I handed the binoculars back to Luke and walked out of the room, letting him go on spying on whoever it was, as long as he wanted. I was just too old for that other house now.

CHAPTER XIII: JOHN BROWN ON TRIAL

O N THE FIRST SATURDAY NIGHT in August, the Richmonds and I piled into their Toyota and headed up High Street. We were off to the big John Brown play! Finally the moment had come. All day, I had been tiptoeing around my parents and brothers, not sure whether they knew the play was tonight or not, waiting every second for one of them to blare out that I was forbidden from going. But the evening came, and no one seemed to know, so I escaped!

As Mr. Richmond steered up the long hill in town, Alex, Luke, and I put on fake mustaches and beards, to look like John Brown's thirty-something-year-old sons. To look dirty-faced, like we had been fighting Union troops, we had a can of stage makeup as brown as shoe polish. As I smeared it down my cheeks, glancing in the visor mirror, Luke and Alex started laughing because I had gotten gobs of it in my eyelashes.

"All in the spirit of authenticity, boys!" Mr. Richmond roared out, warming up his John Brown voice.

By the time we turned onto Philmore Street, Alex, Luke, and I were made up in floppy hats and fake beards, our faces streaked like John Brown's raiders. Daniel, who was playing a rowdy spectator, was decked out in an old-time suit and top hat. If there were any girls at the play, they'd go crazy for him.

Philmore Street was full of the fanciest old houses. Many had big names. Our Lady of Longstreet was a yellow mansion with curvy white columns. McClellan's Charge and Burnside's Brigade were also giant structures. But the house we pulled up to was a stone house not much bigger than the one my family lived in. I had barely noticed it in all these years. There was a high black gate around it, floodlights in the yard, and fancy electric candles in every window. The mortar was as white as the backs of my sneakers, and the columns glistened with green paint. This was my mother's dream home—a small Harpers Ferry limestone house like ours, restored to the hilt!

A chubby man with a pink face and a wineglass in his hand opened the door and was all smiles for Mr. Richmond. He even gave him a big hug like a woman. I recognized him. He was a big-name author around town. He wrote ghost stories about Harpers Ferry and Antietam, the famous battlefield just eleven miles up the road, across the river in Maryland. Was he the man in the play my father hated? The one my mother had warned me about?

"I see you all have come ready," he said, chuckling as he looked around at our different costumes.

We went inside to a room full of bright lights and people

dressed up like on Halloween. Right away my heart began to pound. Around the room were park people who were my neighbors but who never spoke to my family because my brothers had done something bad to them. The man in the farmer's overalls—Jerry had bent the antenna off his Jeep. The man who lived right behind us—Robbie had taken the distributor cap off his VW just to see him try to start it in the morning. The park architect dressed in an old-time suit—Dad didn't like him because he double-parked his Cadillac everywhere on the narrow cobblestone streets. Father Ron was here, toting one of those toy muskets they sold in souvenir shops around town. Dad definitely hated him. Lee Jackson was here wearing an old floppy hat just like mine. I couldn't imagine what part he was playing. He was on Dad's blacklist, too.

As I looked at them all talking and laughing, I began to realize that no one recognized me under my itchy fake mustache and beard. It was like I was at a masquerade ball. When Daniel, Alex, and Luke started laughing and smiling along with Mr. Richmond, who was talking to a group of people, so did I, and for a second, I was rubbing shoulders with Harpers Ferry's upper crust! I wished my scared little parents could see me now, especially Mom. This was nothing. As nice as she was, she could do this easy.

As I found myself glancing around this beautiful house, the ache in my stomach for my mother grew. This was how she wanted our house to look—walls painted bright, chandeliers everywhere, fancy dark furniture, oval rugs, antique lamps, teacups.

Drifting away from everyone, I peeked into the first room I could. Over the fireplace was a big painting of George Washington. We had that exact same painting in our house! Only ours was smaller and in a cheap frame. We had the same fireplace mantel, too. But this one was refinished in fancy red wood and filled with neat candles. Dad had put a rusted stovepipe into our fireplace, which curled down to a potbelly stove some old hillbilly must have stuck his head into and committed suicide a hundred years ago.

I peeked into another room. Wow! A fancy wooden desk big enough for the president. A computer with speakers! In this room in our house, Dad stuck boxes and boxes of old *Popular Mechanics* magazines and left the plaster walls full of cracks. Jerry said it was like *The Addams Family* house in there. We didn't need to build an addition on our house or move up to Ridge Street—we could fix up our house to look just like this one.

I went back out to the main room, where everyone was chatting. After everyone stood around for a while, talking and sipping from wineglasses, Mr. Richmond appeared from a back room, wearing an old nightgown and a phony gray beard much longer and scragglier than mine, along with a white bandage around his forehead, spotted with fake blood. The room quieted down, and everyone took their places. The lights soon dimmed, except for a desk lamp, which was angled to shine on Mr. Richmond's face as he lay on the sofa, looking injured.

A tall man wearing what looked like a Dracula cape came into the room and sat in a fancy chair at the head of the sofa. Behind him was a man holding a nightstick. I recognized him as a park ranger. Behind him was a Civil War soldier, standing like a guard. Two others in dark suits came into the room. Everyone else sat in folding chairs along the wall. The red chairs were for the jury, and the gray ones for the spectators. Some had out playbooks. My heart started pounding.

Then the man in Dracula cape started speaking in a heavy, low tone that sounded like a church organ: "John Brown, you stand accused of treason against the United States." He unrolled a large scroll and read from it. "You stand accused of inciting rebellion, of insurrection . . ." He unrolled the scroll further. ". . . of arson, larceny, and looting—and the severest of these charges, indeed of all charges against man . . ." Letting the scroll roll up on its own, the judge leaned down from his throne and stared an angry face at the injured John Brown. ". . . of murder!"

From the back of the courtroom came a thunder of banging plastic gunstocks.

"Guilty! Guilty! Guilty!" chanted the spectators in the gray chairs. Father Ron, standing tall among them, looked like a madman.

The judge, in swift response to this outburst, banged his gavel until the courtroom quieted. Then the chubby man with the pink face spoke at length, in a funny, overdone voice, pointing a Bible at John Brown: "The accused," he said, "shall be judged by the law of God and the land"—he turned and looked back at the spectators—"and not by prejudice and wrath!"

It went on this way for some time, with everyone getting a chance to point their finger at John Brown, using words like "guilty" and "everlasting punishment." I was totally caught up in the moment, wondering how, as John Brown's son, Frederick Brown, I would die to protect my father. A bayonet to the chest? A gunshot?

Finally, with the bright light from the desk lamp on his face, John Brown sat up and, with his arm outstretched, started speaking to the ceiling in a wavering voice.

". . . I have yet another objection," he said, his long gray beard falling down, "and that is, it is unjust I should suffer such a penalty . . . Had I so interfered in behalf of the rich, the powerful, the intelligent—"

He stamped his bare foot down on the floor, rattling dresser handles all around the room.

"—the so-called great, either father, mother, brother, sister, wife, or children—"

He paused as one by one, Alex, Luke, and I stepped forward, knelt, and placed our hands on his. In the bright light, I saw him look at each of us, his face as chalky as stone. My heart was pounding hard. I never imagined that the moment could feel so great.

"—it would have been all right," he went on, "and every man in this court would have deemed it an act worthy of reward, rather than punishment!"

The courtroom spectators roared in outrage. So much so, the judge banged his gavel, and the Civil War soldier stepped forward and drew his sword, its blade gleaming in the light.

Then, in reverse order, Alex, Luke, and I stepped back, and John Brown went on speaking, saying he was under God's commandment. He spoke in long sentences that rose and fell like mountains and valleys. He said he had no consciousness of guilt and that he regretted the weakness of man. He mentioned places like Missouri and Canada and spoke of trying to free slaves without violence.

When he finished, Lee Jackson, with the light trained on him, stood and spoke, saying the accused was innocent in the eyes of God. Then the light swung on Alex.

"If my father so consecrates his life to the destruction of slavery," he said, "no penalty by man can stand against him for his deed. Not now or ever!"

Luke started speaking before the light reached him— "Who are we as a nation if only some of us should live freely?" He shook his fist at the judge. "The bees of revolution will begin to swarm!"

There were chuckles in the back of the room.

My chest was as hard as an oil drum by the time the spotlight blazed across my bearded face.

"I stand here today," I said, my voice not cracking once, "before God and country, in defense of my father"—I spun around and faced the unruly spectators—"for his actions are brave and of the noblest!"

Muskets rose up in my face. Father Ron's pie-face looked hideous as he shook his plastic gun at me—he should have been in the picture window across from my house, not John Brown. The gavel banged, and banged. The guard drew his nightstick. I felt the eyes of the room searing through me as

I soared over the world, as if planet Earth was a Ferris wheel and I had the highest seat.

The light swung back onto the judge in the black cape, who rambled on for some time about crimes against humanity and their consequences. He spoke for so long that Alex, Luke, and I sat cross-legged on the floor.

"John Brown," he said finally, "it is the pronouncement of this court that you be hanged by the neck until—"

"Mankind will forever dwell in the wilderness of his ignorance," John Brown shouted in one final breath, "'less I forfeit my life for the furtherance of the ends of justice!"

Though injured, he shook his fist fiercely at the judge.

"Hear! Hear!" Daniel cheered loudly, standing in his spiffy suit.

More outbursts, more gavel banging, then more soldiers came into the room.

When the lights came back on, everyone started clapping, smiling, and looking around at one another. Mr. Richmond, the wounded John Brown, stood, pulled off his phony beard, and bowed. He waved Alex, Luke, and me up beside him, and we all bowed and smiled under our fake beards.

The clapping went on forever. In the brightly lit room, the chubby man, raising his wineglass, said he thought it was one of their best plays yet. The smiles went on and on, and for the next hour, we devoured carrot cake and swilled Sprite. In all that time, I absolutely did not know my name, if it wasn't Frederick Brown.

Chapter XIV: Shakespeare's Tears

I was worried crazy by the time the Richmonds and I rode down the hill that night. I had been gone a long time, and it was late. As soon as we pulled up, I hopped out and ran low through the trees to my back door, trying to wipe the makeup off with a handful of tissues. The lights were on in the kitchen, so I sneaked up the back stairs and made it inside and to the bathroom without a noise. But when I ran the water, the pipes groaned, and Mom called up. When I didn't answer, she came up and saw me wiping my face in a hurry.

"What in heaven's name?"

The makeup, caked in the corners of my eyes, had also left streaks on my cheeks and neck. My father, silent as an Indian, appeared behind her, came closer, and turned my head in to the light.

"What the hell is this?" he said.

I stood paralyzed as his fingers pinched my forehead like a giant insect.

"You mean," he said, leaning down in my face, "you went to that damn play after I specifically told you not to?"

"Oh, Josh, how could you?" my mother said.

I felt the sting of his meaty hand across my cheek before I knew it was coming. I reeled back, holding my face.

"You're just jealous of Mr. Richmond!" I shouted, glaring my ugliest face at him.

My voice filled the house, every little room, like a shout trapped in a tin can.

"Katie, you hear this?" he said, turning to her.

"You are!" I shouted, before he could lie and make it seem otherwise. "'Cause I got to defend a real hero!"

My face was all scrunched up. Tears were starting. And the sting on my cheek was only making me angrier.

"A hero?" he said, grinning his flabby jaws at me. "Niles Richmond?"

"No, John Brown!" I roared.

The floor in the hallway creaked—my brothers listening in.

"Get back to bed, you two!" Dad yelled.

He turned back to me, the ugly grin back on his face.

"They *hung* your damn 'hero,' mister. Think about that," he said.

I stood hating him with all my might. I didn't care what he said or how he tried to ruin the moment. He wasn't half the man John Brown was. He was just angry and doing nothing about it. He was the one who should have been made of wax and stuck in a window for my brothers to shoot BBs at, not John Brown.

"At least he wasn't afraid to stand for something!" I said.

He leaned down with an icy grin on his whiskered face, his smelly pipe tobacco breath in my face.

"What did you say, mister?"

"Bill, please," Mom said, her voice trembling.

I backed up, stumbling.

"John Brown's a saint, and you're a madman!" I shouted.

"Katie, are you hearing this?"

"Josh, be quiet!"

"I would die for John Brown, but not for you!" I yelled.

"Oh, you would, would you?" he said, turning and heading for the closet.

"Bill, no, please," Mom said, rushing after him.

"You watch what the hell you wish for, buster," he said, yanking a belt out of the closet, whacking the leather strap across his knee, and heading for me.

"Bill, no!"

I took a deep breath, shut my eyes, and started speaking the only words I could: "I have yet another objection, and that is, it is unjust I should suffer such a penalty . . . Had I so interfered in behalf of the rich, the powerful, the intelligent—"

"Katie, shut him the hell up!"

I opened my eyes to see him pointing the coiled-up belt at me.

"You see Niles's influence now, don't you, Katie?" he roared.

"—every man in this court would have deemed it an act worthy of reward, rather than punishment," I said right in his face.

"I'll show you punishment," he said, drawing the belt back.

"Bill, you're getting yourself all upset!" Mom cried.

"You bet I'm upset! Listen to this nonsense. Niles Richmond has caused enough damn problems, Katie." He pointed the belt at me, coiled in his grip like a whip. "You're not to step foot over there ever again, mister." He came toward me. "You hear me? Never again." He stepped back. "You just fixed your wagon but good, buster. Katie, you hear? Never again."

"Oh, Bill, please."

"No," he said, shaking his head. "No, 'oh Bill please' this time. He's had his chances. That's it." He called up through the floor. "Jerry, Robbie, you hear me? All of you are forbidden from setting foot off this property *for the rest of this summer*—you hear me?"

"Oh, Bill, that's ridiculous."

He spun around.

"Is it? We'll just see," he said, slapping the belt across his leg again.

Mom started pushing me toward the door before King Kong could go any crazier.

"Oh, Josh, how could you?" she said. "No more plays. You can visit with Luke for anything but that."

"The hell he can!" Dad roared behind us. "Absolutely not! No more visiting next door at all, period! For no damn reason. You hear me?"

I turned and leered down the steps at him.

"Nay," I said, pulling my invisible sword, "I must change for the coming day!"

He took a giant step toward me with his belt—"You better change into your damn pajamas, you little SOB!"

I ducked behind Mom and stuck out an ugly face at him. I was not proud of myself. From John Brown's brave son to this, in less than an hour.

I went into the bedroom and climbed into the top bunk, where I lay sniffing and wiping my eyes. Jerry and Robbie lay still in the dark below me. When Mom and Dad went back downstairs, Robbie grumbled first.

"Way to go, Josh."

Jerry gave my mattress a good jolt with his foot.

"'Nay, I must change.' Let's see you change now, asswipe." I started to say something, but he talked right over me—"Cowmint! Cowmint! *Cowshit,* you mean."

It was like that from both of them until I fell asleep.

I WOKE THE NEXT MORNING to the sound of hammering in our backyard. When I ran downstairs, I found Mom peering out our back window.

"Your father," she said, dread in her voice, "is putting up a fence."

A fence? I peered out the window with her to see Dad,

angry-faced, hammering a long post into the ground. A fence between us and the Richmonds!

"See what you did?" she said, turning to me.

I could see every one of my mother's forty-one years whittled out to the end of her nose, and a sick feeling started inside. Everything had gone wrong and was only getting worse. All I did was play John Brown's son. What was so wrong with that?

I wanted to tell Mom about the restored house I had been in last night, about how wonderful it looked even though it was small and cramped like our house, with low ceilings. I wanted to share it with her, like vacation pictures or something. But she hated me now, and there was nothing I could do or say this time to make her kind to me again.

All morning, work on the fence went on. Dad had taken off work just to put it up. He had Jerry and Robbie helping him, hammering down posts and handing him lengths of wire, which he strung and snipped himself. I watched from every window in the house at least once, as the posts marched across our yard and as the strands of wire, one by one, were stretched between them. Every second, I could feel this barbed wire being pulled across my insides. I wondered if John Brown had felt the same way when they hanged him.

At one point, I went downstairs and stood in front of my mother, looking up at her.

"Oh, don't start crying," she said in the cruelest way, shaking her head.

The sound of her giving up on me was too much to bear.

I felt myself rise over the room, like a big blow-up doll of a boy.

"What kind of boy," she went on to say, "intentionally aggravates his father?" She looked off, shaking her head again. "Where did I go wrong?"

She made me so angry I kicked the chair.

"I feel so sorry for you, Josh," she said. "You have a hard life ahead of you."

I ran upstairs, slamming doors—"Go away, ghost! Go away, ghost!" Then I ran into a closet and hid myself, the old dark coat hanging down like the cape of a vampire opening up and swallowing me.

At noon, when Dad came in for lunch, I sat sulking on the back porch, avoiding him. I could hear him yelling below, ranting and raving again about last night, making it clear to Mom that I was *not, not, under no circumstances,* allowed off our property.

"No more Richmonds!" he yelled up through the house. "Josh, you hear me?"

My heart sank and died a hundred times. There was no way around it this time—I had seen the last of the Richmonds' house. No more Luke. No more Mr. Richmond. No more wonderful house.

By late afternoon, the horrible fence was done. Across our yard it marched, a dozen fence posts, spaced evenly across the weeds, with shiny strands of barbed wire stretched supertight between them. On the far side of it sat my cowmint patch, cut off from me for the first time. The jerk even nailed up store-bought orange and black plastic No Trespassing signs, putting them everywhere, so that we and the world *must* see them every step we took.

I was sick inside. A fence between us and the Richmonds.

"Way to go, Josh," Jerry muttered, kicking one of the stout fence posts.

Robbie stood staring far away, so far away that he seemed to look around the world and back at himself. I had never felt we were brothers before, but at that moment, it seemed we were all together on the same side of this new fence—and all together, in not wanting to be where we were.

The worst moment would come that afternoon when Jerry sneaked over the brand-new fence to stomp down my cowmint plants—right before my eyes. By the time I got there, all seven plants lay mashed into oblivion, a thunder of boot marks where the green and purple petals had grown so beautifully. I swung at my brother, only to get shoved down hard. Our screaming and shouting brought Robbie across the fence to break it up.

Sobbing there on the ground, I spilled my guts to my brothers about all that I had overheard from the kitchen window the evening I discovered cowmint, about something following Dad and him needing to go to confession.

"Following him? Confession?" Jerry said, hissing the word down at me. "Dad?"

"Crying?" echoed Robbie. "That old bastard never cries."

"Swear. It was over Grandma's house or something," I sobbed. "And remember that old picture of the priest in our photo album? It's gone now!"

But they didn't believe me. Left in my decimated cow-mint patch, I knew what John Brown would do. He'd burn my house to the ground, for no reason other than rage.

Jerry was cruel for hours. I found pieces of my murdered plants in my bed, even stuck down my slot in the toothbrush holder.

"Mama-mama, mama-mama, somebody stomped them all down!" he cried out, making fun of me, plucking the head off a limp plant and popping me in the face with it.

Supper passed horribly, and the evening was no better. No one was talking, and the house was quiet. Dad wouldn't even let us turn on the TV. At one point, I heard knocking on the front door. I sat up in bed and listened. Who was it? It seemed weird to me that of all the people in the world, I hoped Ricky Hardaway was coming to see me. "Hi, Bill, you SOB," I could see him saying, before pouring back a Coke. Instead, I heard Luke's voice. Dad, though, sent him away. After that, the only sound in the house was the church bells next door. I sat up in my bunk, looking across the street at the wax figure of John Brown, a million things going wild in my mind.

For one great moment last night, I had been John Brown's son, and despite this new fence across our yard, that moment still glowed in me. Mr. Richmond had been my father, and my life had felt right.

I LAY AWAKE HALF the night. Damn my father! In my mind, the charges against him were as lengthy as those against John Brown—"Bill Connors, you stand accused of unneighborliness," I could hear a judge saying.

If I were a judge and I had a scroll of charges, I'd unroll them before my father and say, "Dad, you stand accused of treason against the National Park Service, of inciting rebellion in your children and the destruction of park property. You stand accused of meanness, of anger that does no good, of name-calling of park officials, of making your sons unhappy—and the severest of these charges—of being a plain old miserable, grumpy jerk."

And just as the world had found John Brown guilty, so they would find my father guilty.

Guilty! Guilty! Guilty!

I could see the townspeople today banging their plastic gunstocks.

"*Bill Connors,* you invite no one into your house. *Bill Connors,* you don't wave, blow your horn, or smile. All you do is shut your doors and draw your blinds."

Guilty! Guilty! Guilty!

I lay back on my bed and looked up at the cracked ceiling. How could the greatest moment of my life have come crashing to earth this way? In the dark night, I could even hear Shakespeare laughing. Or crying—I couldn't be sure which.

CHAPTER XV: THE SILVER PAINT INCIDENT

THE NEXT MORNING, I SAT on the back porch until I heard my father's car start for work. Then I got up and wandered through my cluttered backyard, eyeing the new barbed-wire fence that looked all the more savage and terrible in the morning light. The strands were so shiny they looked electrified. I wouldn't put it past him.

Then my eyes fell on old paint can after old paint can tossed into the weeds. There was black paint, blue, some white. One can was splattered with silver paint. My packrat father had saved all these cans for some reason. When I spotted our perfectly good ladder lying in the weeds, I stopped to look up through the buggy sunshine at our ugly rusted roof.

"Man lives in a wilderness of ignorance," John Brown had said.

I glanced all around my yard. I sure knew what John Brown would do if he were growing up in this house. He'd tear down this wilderness. But my thoughts were going somewhere else.

As soon as I heard Mom's car leave for the store, as quietly as I could, I dug the aluminum ladder out of the weeds and raised it up against the back of the house. From the weeds, I grabbed up the can of silver paint, finding a second can of silver paint. Two cans. Even better. I found a decent brush in the toolshed, along with a screwdriver, and, after shaking up both cans, popped the lid off one. Rich, bubbly silver paint appeared. When I popped the lid off the second can, the paint looked funny—runny, streaky, full of bluish swirls. *I probably shouldn't use that paint,* I told myself. Using baler twine, I tied the paintbrush to the end of a broomstick and, with the can of good paint in one hand and my sword-long brush in the other, started up the ladder.

Step after step, I rose up the back of our house, my eyes soon level with the tops of the upstairs windows. I could see inside our house, the cluttered corners and old floors. I could see all around the outside of the house, too—Jerry's good Nerf ball in the rain gutter beside me and wasps' nests under the eaves. I felt I was looking our ugly old home right in the eye.

After hooking the handle of the paint can over a snow guard. I loaded the superlong brush with silver paint, reached up into the middle of the roof as far as I could, and soaked the heart of the ugly rust stain in one swipe. A second time, a third time, a fourth, again and again I brushed the paint up and down, back and across, working it to perfection, growing excited as the syrupy silver paint soothed the hideous spot like a cream.

But after just a dozen or so thrusts with the broomstick, the paintbrush drooped loose. At the same time, I wiggled the ladder—sending it tipping. Before I knew it, down I went. I landed on my feet on the soft ground, but the ladder hit a pile of cinder blocks nearby and made a terrific bang that echoed up and down the sides of every house on the street. I glanced around wildly as I waited for my brothers to come flying out of the house. But they didn't.

Quickly, I set up the ladder again, retied the paintbrush to the broomstick, and, after picking leaves and sticks out of the wet bristles, climbed back up. This time, as I spread the silver paint far in every direction, I was careful to keep my balance. Still, I had to work fast, as I had a whole roof to paint before my parents came home.

Brushful after brushful, I reached and stretched to spread the paint as far as possible, my heart pounding, my eyes flashing, my every muscle working to cover the sun-scorched, rusted roof with a bright silver shine. Soon I had much of it covered, and it was so beautiful to see. I couldn't believe it. Just like that, after all these years of having to look at this ugly rust spot, to know it was there for the world to see no matter how far down I held my head, I was getting rid of it! Just like that, on a morning that could have been any other morning, I was giving my family a brand-new, sparkling roof—with just a few strokes of a brush and some leftover paint!

We did belong in Harpers Ferry. We did! If all it took was paint from this can, we did. After all, we had a two-hundred-year-old armory worker's house. If that wasn't historical enough, I didn't know what was.

Boy, wouldn't Dad be surprised this evening. After another long, hard day on the mail route, he'd come home, look up, and see this brand spanking new roof. Cowmint was nothing compared to this! He'd be happy this time for sure.

Oh, sure, he'd yell at me. He'd even make a big show of being unhappy about it. But when he saw how beautiful our roof looked and how happy Mom was smiling up at it, all while the roof beamed down at my family like God's smile, my father would finally look at me the way Mr. Richmond had looked at him when he told the cowmint story so long ago, it seemed.

Up and down the roof I spread the paint, stopping only to catch runs or to move the ladder so that I could reach more of the roof. At one point, I glanced over my shoulder at Jefferson's Rock in the distance. Out on the ledge were colorfully dressed tourists, and someone in blue was waving to me. Was it Luke? As I waved back, I felt I was changing history by attacking the big rust stain on our roof, and whoever was on Jefferson's Rock seemed to know.

"Nay, I must change for the coming day," I said to myself, raising my broomstick overhead.

Caught up in the moment, I turned on the ladder to wave my broomstick like a sword to all the windows in the

Richmonds' house. Then I turned and, for the heck of it, waved it up at the gold cross on St. Peter's. Next thing I knew, the ladder kicked out, and down I went again! This time, the paint can went flying through the air, splashing a big silver streak across Mom's good ferns and marigolds. The ladder banged against the same pile of cinder blocks, sounding like the London Bridge was falling down in my backyard. Out the back door came Jerry.

"What the hell are you doing?" he shouted, gaping around at the silver splatter all over the ground.

Before he could stop me, I stood the ladder up again, grabbed the can of paint, along with the broomstick brush, and started scampering back up. This time, instead of standing on the top rung, I climbed out on the roof and wedged my sneaks between the raised seams in the tin. Untying the twine and letting the broomstick roll down into the rain gutter, I seized hold of the sloppy paintbrush by its short handle and started flapping the sparkling silver paint up and back, faster and faster, all while ignoring my brother's shouts from below.

But the harder I brushed, for some reason, the runnier the paint became. Soon it was bubbling and streaking all over. No matter how much paint I slopped from the can and slung across the roof, it kept thinning and oozing down like melted cake icing.

I stopped and looked around. What in the heck was going on? The bristles of my brush were soaked up to the handle, and paint was halfway up my arms. I heard Jerry yelling up at me.

"It's full of paint thinner, you idiot!" he roared. "You got the wrong freakin' can!"

Paint thinner? I looked around in terror. Oh, no. He was right! Somehow in all the falling, I had gotten the good paint can mixed up with the bad, which was like water. I couldn't believe it—the whole roof was streaking, and the rust stain was bleeding through, laughing its ugly face at me. I peered down into the can. Full of bubbles! I dipped my brush in and swished it around the liquidy paint—stuff ran off the bristles like silver milk.

I knew enough handyman stuff to know that I had contaminated the whole roof, that there was no way to get the paint thinner off, not without hosing down our house with kerosene. In one stupid, desperate effort, I slung the rest of the bad paint across the roof—but it just washed down into the gutter like superfreaky acid rain.

I was dead.

Letting both brush and can drop to the ground, I retreated down the ladder, all while Jerry pelted me with sticks and shouted in my ear. Once on the ground, I started kicking weeds and scuffing the dirt, trying to hide the big silver splashes across our backyard. But the mess was everywhere— on leaves, flowers, rocks, tree trunks, even splattered across piles of rusted junk. It looked like the Tin Man had been mutilated in our backyard!

But my horror was only starting. Jerry was shouting again, pointing up. I looked up to see our house sweating silver paint! Large paint drops were beading the full length of our rain gutter, lining up like atom bombs to fall today, tomorrow, next week, and all next year—a million silver drops, large and swollen, to drip off our roof for the next hundred years!

Jerry was running around, freaking out. Robbie, finally hearing the commotion, came barreling out the back door, stopped, and stood gawking up, half a Twinkie stuffed in his fat face.

Grabbing dirty rags out of the toolshed, I clambered back up the shaky ladder and started wiping down the wet roof. But the silver paint, now tacky in spots, while still runny in others, began smearing everywhere and gunking up under my rag like paste. I couldn't believe what was happening. The paint I had so lovingly put on was now coming off in my hands like overcooked chicken skin. I looked down at my brother, the tears starting.

"Oh, you're dead, doofus," he said. "You're dead, dead, dead."

How could it get any worse? But it did. When I again tried wiping off the roof, the paint thinner in the paint mixed with the motor oil on the dirty rags and made long, black streaks down the middle of our roof, turning the top of my house into a giant zebra.

"Oh, you're really dead!" Jerry was saying, backing up, shaking his head. "You're definitely really dead."

Definitely really dead? Why didn't God just send a thunderbolt through our house and get it over with? Better yet, have the steeple topple on us! Robbie, no help at all, stood there with Twinkie cream on his face.

I shimmied down the ladder, ran around like a nut, only

to fling in anger the messy paintbrush high into the air, then watch it land smack-dab in the center of the roof—thump!—and stick there. The only thing to stick to our rotten roof was the cockamamie paintbrush.

Disgusted, I kicked over the ladder and stood back watching it fall, only to see it get hung up in a limb, the treetops rustling under its weight. Again and again I kicked the ladder, trying to send it down to the ground. But the stupid rungs held on to the high branches, refusing to let go. I started yanking on the ladder, shaking the treetops over my house like King Kong, sending down leaves and paint drops on my head. I was out of my mind—muttering, screaming, and crying. Over and over I jerked on the ladder, trying to get it unstuck. Then, *crack!*

I looked up in horror to see a large limb breaking off. As it dropped and dangled down, hanging by a shred of bark, sunlight poured in, lighting up the dark, silver-spotted ground, lighting up the rust-orange junk piles—lighting the whole side of our rotten ugly house! Time stopped. For the first time in a hundred years, our moldy old stone house stood naked in sunbeams. I waited for it to turn to ash and crumble down like sunlit Dracula himself.

Jerry ran mad around the yard, stopping to punch me in the shoulder and tell me I was dead a hundred times over. Robbie still stood there with Twinkie cream on his cheek, looking stunned. All the while, the biggest stage light in creation shined on the mess I had made of our home. Now, from clear up on Jefferson's Rock to the grassy knoll across the street, a half-million tourists a year could see the worst of it: the dirty plastic covering our windows, the gnarly white extension cord holding up the rain gutter, and the tattered tar paper and strips of pink insulation from where Dad never finished the back porch. On top of that, the sky was raining watery silver paint down our roof, while the rust spot reared its ugly head at me once again. I stood in the middle of King Kong's demolished island, my arms bruised and scraped up. *Drip . . . drip . . . drip.* I was dead.

Then, incredibly, from high above came church bells. *Dong! Dong! Dong!* I looked up at the steeple of St. Peter's thundering down on the far side of our house. I couldn't run through the barbed-wire fence to escape to the Richmonds' anymore, but I could run down the long shadow of the steeple to the church next door. There was one person left in the world for me to go to. Father Ron. He had invited me over as the church's official cowmint expert.

I started running for the church, then skidded to a stop in our junky yard. No, Ricky! He was the one person who could help me. He could fix our roof, our whole house for that matter.

I stood looking down, confused. In one great insane moment, I saw both the priest of St. Peter's and my long-haired cousin, the two of them in flannel shirts and blue jeans, saving me.

CHAPTER XVI: FATHER RON

I WASHED MYSELF OFF AS BEST I could and dashed down the alley toward the church. By the time I reached the stone walk that curved through the grassy grounds, I was on autopilot, running, I felt, to my last place on earth. Up the steps and through the giant archway I went. Opening the big door, I found the church dark inside except for a few candles burning around the altar, making blurry orange haloes around the one or two heads in the front pews. Behind me, the big door latched with a high echo. I glanced off to the left, at the statue of the Virgin Mary glowing blue in the chapel, then off to the right, at the confessional, above which the green light, thank God, was on.

I stepped up to the holy water font and dipped my fingers in, then stopped—I had forgotten which way to cross myself, to the left or right. I looked around, worried someone was watching. Fudging it with a halfhearted cross, I headed for the dark curtain over the confessional and stepped through beneath the green light.

In the dim light I let in, I saw Father Ron behind the metal screen. He was gazing off into nowhere, like one of those religious faces in ancient, cracked-up Italian paintings.

"Son," he said.

I wondered if he recognized me, or if this was his standard hello for all boys. I had not forgotten that I was the church's official cowmint expert, but that little honorary title was kid stuff at the moment. When I knelt, the weight of my knees made the kneeler creak. The swaying curtain behind me soon stilled, and the slivers of light bouncing in and out stopped. Pitch blackness swallowed me up. Thus began my darkest moment.

"Bless me, Father," I began, in a scratchy, scared voice, "for I have sinned. It has been—"

I did not really pause, but it felt like I did, like I was fibbing to start my confession.

"—three years since my last confession. During that time—"

Then I did pause, to take a deep breath. With my voice going higher, faster, and louder, I spilled it all. I told him that my father had put up a fence between us and the Richmonds, that my brother had stomped down all my cowmint plants, then how I had made a mess of our roof and broken off a large limb—and now our ugly house was wide open for tourists to gawk at.

Not that I had in mind that Father Ron could tell me how to fix the roof like the Home Depot guy or how to glue the rotten tree back together, but I was disappointed when he started asking me stupid questions: why my brothers weren't with me, if my father was planning on returning to church, and if I had missed the church. I had the feeling he had been waiting for this day and even practicing. He reminded me that my brothers and I still hadn't been confirmed or received First Communion. Then he said words like "turmoil" and "strife" and "everlasting commitment to God" until I realized he was talking about my family.

"It's because of Grandma's old house!" I said in one desperate shot.

"The fellowship of God requires . . ." The wooden bench on his side of the metal screen creaked. "Your grandmother's house?"

"The big white caretaker's house on River Road," I said. "At the old church retreat my grandparents were the caretakers of."

I heard him sit up.

"You mean the old Marist retreat?" he asked.

I was glad he knew about it. He even called it by its official name.

"He always gets upset about it," I said.

I could hear him lean closer to the metal screen, the wooden bench on his side creaking.

"Do you know why that is?" he asked.

My body went stiff from the knees up, causing the kneeler under me to pop. I knew my father was angry with the church for letting the Catholic retreat go to ruin. I knew that in his heart he was sick over the fact that the chapel and grounds had been looted bare. I also knew he was sad that the big white house now stood empty. And I had always known he was all-around unhappy. But I also knew there was something more.

"No," I heard myself answering.

"Oh."

I could hear the disappointment in his voice. But I was determined to show him I was no dumb kid.

"But Mom said he should come see you."

"And did she say *why*?"

This was the moment of truth, and my knees were on the kneeler pad like sneaks squarely on bike pedals.

"She said something was following Dad."

I could feel the confessional throw its dark curtains around us, keeping the world out.

"What . . . is following your father?" he asked.

When I didn't answer, he spoke again, sounding a little impatient.

"Son, did your mother say what specifically is . . . bothering him?"

For a second, I thought I'd just come out and tell him. "Mom said he thinks you're somebody else." Briefly, I was even prepared to tell him about the picture in our photo album of the priest who might, or might not, look like him, a picture now missing.

Instead, a blunt question of another kind just came out of me: "Was your father a priest?"

When he was quiet for a moment, I was sure I had hit detective pay dirt.

"No," he finally said, with a chuckle in his voice, "he was a high school social studies teacher."

"Oh."

"Why?"

I could feel myself tumbling into the dark, all the more foolish. But before I knew it, my eyes were welling up with tears, and out it all came—my kooky art, my kooky cowmint, the John Brown play, the stolen church items. Talking in every direction, I made no sense. My voice bounced off the black curtains like a batty moth.

"Dad hates me!" I finally cried out.

"Son, no," Father Ron said, "your father doesn't hate you. Please, you mustn't believe that. Your father has simply lost his faith."

I felt my body collapse on the kneeler, where I started sobbing in the dark, nodding as if I understood.

"But why? Mr. Richmond was impressed by him," I cried.

"Yes, Niles, is very—" Father Ron broke off and was silent for a moment. "Impressed how?" he asked.

"For finding cowmint."

"But I thought *you* found that plant."

"Well . . . we both did."

It seemed the easiest way to clear it up. I heard his bench creak again.

"Josh, your plant is a beautiful discovery. But sometimes faith . . . requires more than a plant. It's a belief. It's something that withstands time. Well, like a house. Some houses are weather-beaten, but some are bright and new. You—*we*—must pray for your father."

He told me I must honor and obey my parents and gave

me as penance five Hail Marys and five Our Fathers. This was standard. He went on about understanding and forgiveness, and though honestly I did feel better, I was hoping for more from him. For one fantastic moment I again saw him in a flannel shirt and blue jeans, helping me paint my roof.

Then, in the darkness of the confessional, I heard myself ask a Catholic priest a question I never thought I would.

"Can Ricky help us with the roof?"

"Ricky? I'm sure he'd be happy to. Why don't you ask him? He was out back a while ago, working in our gardens. Check there."

As I started to leave the confessional, letting in light through the bulky curtain, Father Ron stopped me, his face close to the screen.

"Josh, you're always welcome in God's church. Remember that."

He handed me something. In the dim light I saw that it was a donation envelope, but he handed it to me like his business card.

"Be courageous, son," he said.

Back in the pew, I shut my eyes and prayed for everything good—for my father, for my family, for all I could. But I knew I would need more than prayers.

What I needed was Ricky to fix our stupid roof! I hurried out of the pew and on outside. When I cut around to the back of the church, I found a mulch bag on the slate walk. I followed a line of rakes and hoes and more mulch bags to where, in the blinding sunlight, there was a beautiful flower bed. Red and yellow flowers grew high in all directions. Mom would be impressed.

But no Ricky. I looked all over for him, too. I checked down on Potomac Street, over on Shenandoah Street, even up on Jefferson's Rock. Anywhere he could smoke a cigarette and lie to a tourist girl. Everywhere except the Richmonds'. That I couldn't do anymore.

CHAPTER XVII: LOST FAITH

I CAME HOME THAT AFTERNOON TO the worst argument I ever heard my family in. Dad was yelling all over the house about the silver paint dripping off the roof. Jerry, seeing me come in, started blaming me. Robbie did, too. At the same time, Mom was blaming our father for the condition of our house in the first place.

Dad pivoted and put his sights on me.

"Where've you been, you little troublemaker?" he growled. "There's hell to pay for what you did to my roof!"

He glanced down and, before I could think to hide it, spotted the St. Peter's donation envelope still in my hand. Searching for Ricky, I had carried it all over town like God's business card. Now it was wrinkled up and sweaty, but not enough to dissolve away into nothing. Dad stepped up to me and snatched it from my fingers, then held it up so that the whole room could see the big blue cross of St. Peter's on the front, along with the words, "Give To Your Faith."

I waited for him to explode. Instead, he calmly flipped the envelope over, as if examining it.

"Okay, where'd you get this, buster?" he said.

I stood with all of Father Ron's courage in my heart.

"I went to confession," I said outright.

"You went to—"

The breath just went out of him. Mom had to finish.

"Josh, you went over to the church?" she said, trying to point her finger through our limestone wall, her mouth so wide you could have tossed a pumpkin pie through it.

My brothers, meanwhile, just stood there, their dumb heads swiveling back and forth, looking for an explanation. Dad, having recovered from his shock, came over to me in one giant step, his face hatcheted with lines, his neck hopping with veins. I braced for impact. One backhand this close would send my head through the Milky Way. Instead, he grabbed my hand in a fierce grip and held it up for everyone to see.

"You touched that so-called holy water over there with this damn hand?" he roared.

The anger on his face made two of John Brown.

"Bill, please!" Mom cried out.

He flung my hand down and turned to her.

"Katie, this damn boy of ours was in that confessional with Father Ron!"

"Bill," she said, rushing over to him, "it's not what you think. Please."

He whirled around to me.

"Go wash it!" he said, pointing at my hand, then pointing me into the kitchen.

I stood gawking at him. If I didn't know better, I'd say my father was scared.

"Go!"

When I still didn't move, he kicked me in the rump, sending me stumbling into the kitchen. Then he came in after me, looking monsterlike under the low yellow light. Quickly I turned to the sink, spun the faucet on full, and put my hands under the cold blast.

"Soap," he ordered. "Use soap!"

I grabbed the sliver of Ivory and washed like I never had. I was too scared to be angry.

"Who in the hell gave you permission!" he shouted. He leaned down close to me, his pipe tobacco breath in my face. "You didn't take communion, did you?"

"Bill, please!"

"Dad, stop!" Jerry shouted.

Robbie yelled at him, too. And with the three of them yelling at him, he stepped back and stood in the doorway.

"Wash!" he ordered again, pointing my hands into the sink.

From the doorway, he launched into a smattering of paranoid questions—Who else was in the church? Who exactly saw me? He wanted names.

"Father Ron invited me!" I turned and cried out at the top of my lungs.

An ugly, smirking grin came over his face. "Invited you? Invited you how?"

I looked around him at Mom.

"He made me the cowmint expert, Mom!"

"The what?" she said. "Oh, Josh, you're not making any sense."

"Of course he's not."

I tried to explain how Father Ron had made me the cow-mint expert, but they didn't want to listen.

"Wash!" was all Dad said.

With water spraying all over the place and soap lathering up and down both my arms, I stood glaring at my father as he stood glaring back through the doorway at me. I was fed up with him hating the world, with his meanness that did no good. He couldn't even go to confession when he needed to. I did.

I found myself hating him more than ever at that moment. He thought he was washing away just holy water from my hand, but he was making me wash away much more. To think he had tried to help me draw. I wanted to wash my hand a thousand times to get rid of his touch. I'd never draw again because of him!

Suddenly, the words just came out of me, in one full blast, like water from the faucet—"You didn't always hate the church. You lost your faith!"

The old bastard came to a dead stop. For a moment, it was just him and me in the world. No fighting, no yelling, just a strange, big silence, as if we were on top of a Ferris wheel together. It was like that years ago when he made me shoot a rabbit on a hunting trip. It was like that again when he thought my cowmint plant was barberry, then gooseberry, before he finally smelled mint. It would always be that way whenever I was making a stand not to be like him.

Then he stepped toward me again, his neck filled with whopper-sized veins, his face knotted up like a piece of hickory, his shadow climbing the wall around me. I could hear the wheezing of his lungs as he took a deep breath and said, "You just wait till you have your faith tested by a kid who never listens."

"At least Mr. Richmond believes in cowmint!" I shrieked back. It was the only thing I could think to say.

"Is that so?" he said, dropping his hands on his hips.

"And he has a good job with the park!"

"Katie, you hear your son?"

"And he doesn't hit us!"

Dad pointed his finger at me. "Katie, this damn boy of yours is *enamored* with that man."

Like a compass, he ended up pointing in the direction of the wax figure of John Brown across the street. Over the years, he must have pointed in that direction a thousand times, blaming John Brown for everything from the noisy crowds to the costly restoration of Storer College. Given my recent involvement in the John Brown play, it was enough to cross Mom up at this moment.

"Bill, he's not 'enamored'—which man?"

Our father laughed his hyena laugh that came out when the world was too ridiculous to deal with.

Jerry, pitching in against him, blurted out, "Ha! Dad's jealous of John Brown!"

In a low, deadly voice, our father proceeded to say it would be a cold day in hell before he'd be jealous of a treason-hearted Calvinist.

"At least John Brown did something with his life!" I shouted.

In that second, I caught sight of myself in the only crappy little mirror in our house, and my face was nothing any mirror should ever show.

"If Mr. Richmond had Grandma's house, he'd be happy there!" I yelled.

Dad yanked off his belt so hard it whistled through his loops, a sure sign he had had enough.

"He'd put things in all those rooms!" I yelled while I still had the chance.

"Get upstairs!"

"And he'd grow cowmint everywhere!"

"Get!"

"*Cowmint! Cowmint! Cowmint!* And he wouldn't let the church take anything away from him, either!"

With the water still running and soap all over my hands, I scrambled for my life up the stairs and out the back door.

CHAPTER XVIII: MAYHEM ON THE STREETS OF HARPERS FERRY

THAT NIGHT, MY BROTHERS were hellions, and I was, too, right along beside them. With Dad having run off in a huff hours ago and Mom having done the same sometime later, the house was left for us to kick chairs and stomp around in, our fists clenched.

Jerry was blaming Ricky because he couldn't think of anyone else to blame, other than me. Ricky messed around Grandma's old house, stealing the chapel bell and riling Dad. Next thing I knew my brothers were shoving each other. Robbie's back hit the living room wall with such a wallop he knocked the flower vase off the mantel, and water spilled down all over the sofa cushions. Jerry, laughing hard, stomped his big boots down on the loose floorboards in the hall. He hated our old house. He hated Dad, too. All his rules. *No one allowed in, no one allowed out.* We were prisoners, fenced in now. *Keep the doors closed. Don't attract attention.* All because Dad hated the world.

I pulled a drawing pencil out of my pocket, thrust it

overhead as I had my invisible sword, and said, neighing like a horse, "*Naaay,* I must change!"

"*Can't* change, you idiot!" Jerry yelled back.

"Can't change!" I said, jumping up and down on the sofa.

Seeing my brothers roll with laughter was worth any sick feeling I had inside. It was great to be on their side for once.

Jerry, in all the commotion, went over to the bookcase and started rifling through the photo albums, looking for the old picture of the mysterious priest. Faded black-and-whites of Dad's side of the family spilled out everywhere, on the table, on the floor. One got stepped on. Among them were pictures of the white house, the house itself sharp-edged in the sunlight, perfectly rectangular, superwhite, glowing as if alive. Pictures dated 1972 and 1969. One was 1953.

"Damn, it never falls down, does it?" said Robbie.

"I wish the hell it would," said Jerry.

"Hey, we can burn it down," I said.

My brothers turned and looked at me. I was as surprised as they were by what I'd said.

"Remember riding out there?" Jerry asked, looking down at a picture.

My mind went back to the years when we would visit Grandma, Dad's little car bouncing up the wooded lane. Even then, underbrush and vines had started taking over. The Catholic Brothers were everywhere between the dormitories and the chapel, in their close-fitting black pants and shirts, walking in the green woods.

Nostalgia over, Jerry started flinging the snapshots

around the living room like a stacked deck of cards. Need-ing something to destroy, I snapped my good drawing pen-cil and threw it on the floor. That sent the three of us in motion, running helter-skelter through the house, break-ing up anything that could be used as a sword—kite sticks, bamboo fishing poles. I even broke up Mom's good sewing yardstick.

I ran upstairs, spotted Jerry's BB gun in the corner, grabbed it, and climbed up into my bunk. There I lay across my bed, peering down the barrel at the streets of Harpers Ferry like a deadly sniper. Taking the screen off the window for a clearer view, I aimed at the flickering gaslights, at the candles in the windows of the Frederick Douglass House, then up at the moon, the stars, even at a campfire on the mountaintop. Finally, I squared my sights across the street, right on John Brown's forehead. His ugly face had snarled at me for the last time.

"I stand here today, before God and country, in defense of my father, for his actions are brave and of the noblest!"

Ha! I had no father. Not Mr. Richmond. Not John Brown. And not that bastard who made me wash holy water off my hands!

"Ba-boom."

I touched the trigger—and it fired. It fired? It was loaded? I felt the light kick of the spring-loaded gun, heard the whiff of air, and saw the jump of the barrel before my eyes. Oh my God, it was cocked, too? Then I watched in horror as the whole glass front of the picture window across the street shattered and fell like a waterfall of glass, crashing and tinkling all over the sidewalk, like a million marbles running all over. In that same instant, the figure of John Brown tipped forward, slipped down off its base, and fell face-first right down on the sharp points of the street railing. There it stuck, stabbed through the neck, the musket still glued to its wax hands, bouncing ever so slightly until coming to a rest.

I lay frozen across my bed, the street quiet, indeed the whole world silent. I waited for an alarm to ring, for someone on the street to cry out, for a police siren to come wailing down the hill.

Jerry came pounding up the steps. I looked down at him from my sniper's nest.

"It just broke," I said.

He ran to the window and gaped out.

"Josh, you busted it?" he said, sounding like a goody two-shoes for the first time in his life.

I stared at him. How dare he act all innocent. He had been peppering the glass with BBs all his life, putting a million tiny cracks in it. No wonder the glass finally broke, cleaved like a crystal.

"Man, you're in trouble now," he said, making it clear that my BB was the one and only to ever hit the glass.

A wave of sickness came over me inside. I would get blamed, not Jerry. I felt myself starting to whimper.

Think, Josh, think! Quickly I unscrewed the end of the barrel and poured out all the BBs onto the bed. Since it was empty now, I could claim I had thought it was empty all along.

Robbie came running upstairs at the same time I clambered down from my sniper's perch, where I had left a pile of BBs hidden under my pillow.

"Shh," he said to both Jerry and me as he peered out the window. "Somebody's out there." After a moment, he turned to me, a blank look on his face. "It's Luke."

In a trance, I stumbled downstairs and stepped out of my house and down the front steps, unaware that the BB gun was still in my hands. Luke stood in the middle of the street, looking at the brutally shot body of John Brown, dangling down through the jagged glass shards sticking out of the big picture window. Up the street, the Richmonds' lights were on, but their car was not in the driveway. There were no tourists out. I stepped up behind Luke, watching him look at his fallen hero, at Brown's majestic bearded face stabbed by the points of the iron railing. Worse than that, all six feet two inches of him lay unceremoniously dunked headfirst onto the sidewalk, looking dragged out of the window like last season's worn-out mannequin.

When Luke turned to see me holding the gun, his eyes quickly steamed with anger. I could see the shine of rage through his wire-frame glasses as he looked at my fingers on the gunstock, then at the sweat of guilt on my face.

"It was an accident," I said.

But he glared at me all the more. At the same time, he stood lined up with the busted picture window, looking like he was volunteering to take John Brown's place standing in the big window and snarling at my house forever.

"You're just like your stupid jerk father!" he hissed at me.

I felt myself coil up inside. *Like my stupid jerk father, huh?* Fine. If he wanted to hate me, then I wanted to hate him back. Suddenly, everything about him that had bugged me came out, starting with all the bad things I had ever said about my family, the whirlpool I had been stuck in for so long, making fun of my father, all just to get him to laugh. For what?

He never once said anything bad about his brothers. He never once said he even missed his mother, even though I knew he had to. He was just this perfect kid, day in and day out.

I had shown him everything in my life—Grandma's empty house upriver, the ugly backside of my own house. I had told him all the horrible secrets in my family, and he never once said squat.

No kid should be so cool. He already had the father to die for. Why couldn't I at least have the mother to die for or something? But he didn't even need a mother.

Like my stupid jerk father, huh?

Looking at the hate now in his eyes, I did something I would remember for the rest of my life. I raised the BB gun and aimed it right at him. I knew it was empty. I just wanted to scare him good.

"You think you're so perfect," I said.

It was hardly what I wanted to say, but it was all that came out. When he turned and started running, I pulled the trigger. Just like that, I pulled the trigger! The gun jumped in my hands, making its spring-action air-driven sound. Under the old-time streetlight, Luke wheeled around and gaped at me in total astonishment.

I was standing a few steps uphill of him, as he had run downhill, away from his house, cutting off his escape home. Enjoying seeing the fear on his face, I cocked and shot air at him again, and again, and again, until the skinny little jerk, his face full of shock, disappeared into the darkness of the street. Madder and madder, I fired a few more fake shots after him for good measure.

Jerry and Robbie came running out of the house, wondering what was going on. At the same time, Daniel and Alex came trotting down the sidewalk from their house, having heard the crash of the window and now looking for Luke. When they saw John Brown's assassinated body toppled out of the picture window, glass all over the sidewalk, and me standing there with a BB gun, they put two and two together. Making matters worse, Luke, far down the street, cried out, "Daniel, he shot at me!"

Daniel's face went hard with anger.

"You guys are crazy," he said.

Right there in the street, he and Jerry started shoving each other. Jerry, being taller and meaner, soon had the advantage. Robbie, turning on Alex, pushed him over like a tomato stake and quickly had him in a scissors hold on the hard asphalt. Alex, wiggling and screaming, looked stuck down the mouth of a shark. When Daniel yelled at Jerry to stop, Jerry punched him right in the eye. Daniel bent over, blinded. With my brothers and me having the uphill side of the street cut off, Daniel and Alex couldn't just run home. So Daniel jogged off downhill, away from his house, holding his eye. That left Alex to our mercy. Robbie let him up, and Alex started backing up, his hands protecting his face as I raised the BB gun on him, too. Everything was out of control, the moment as wild as the dark night. When he turned to run, I pretended to shoot him in the butt. Robbie grabbed the BB gun from me and cocked and fired a few times for himself, even though he had to know the gun was empty, with no BBs rolling around inside the barrel. All the while, my brothers and I called Alex fag and queer and butt boy, then started chasing both him and Daniel down High Street.

We ended up down on Hog Alley, but the Richmonds were nowhere in sight, having disappeared into the night. What was in sight, though, was Ricky Hardaway's shack. It was a crappy little house made of blue plywood. Tonight it was dark, but Jerry had an idea where Ricky was. Sure enough, taking the path from his house to the river, we found him five minutes later down at The Point, night fishing. The glow of his lantern bathed the riverbank. He was holding a fishing pole, while set up on the ground next to him was a second pole. Nearby was another guy with long hair, surely one of Ricky's drug buddies. We couldn't make out his face. On a cooler was a six-pack.

Peering down over the rock wall, we watched them for a moment.

"Creep stole the chapel bell," Jerry muttered. "He started all this."

Before I knew it, my brother had filled his fists with stones and was throwing them down on Ricky. He grabbed handful after handful and started flinging high and low. Robbie dropped the BB gun and started chucking stones, too. I was backing up from the wall. Enough was enough. But my crazy brothers weren't stopping. Stones were hitting the river, dinging off the lantern, and raining down on the bank. Ricky and the other guy yelled out, dropped their poles, and covered up as they ran down the bank. I kept stepping back from the wall, wanting to run away. But my brothers stayed to toss, dump, and roll the biggest stones they could find over the wall, crushing Ricky's cooler and knocking over his lantern, which winked out, leaving the bank in blackness.

Then the three of us dashed like mad past John Brown's Fort and down the wood-chip trail back toward town. At the trestles we stopped to catch our breath and stood waiting for Ricky's and the other guy's shadows to cross Potomac Street, coming after us. But moment after moment passed, and they didn't.

"They could be circling around," Robbie whispered.

We waited a moment longer, then started slowly on down the trail. Where Shenandoah and Potomac streets came together, we ran into the Richmonds coming out of their hiding spots in the dark town, trying to sneak home. The six of us stood facing off in the street, our shadows coming together in one big blob. It was the one time you couldn't tell us apart.

Daniel was shouting at us, saying we were nuts. Jerry

was laughing at him, calling him and his brothers wusses and puds. Alex looked scared to death of the BB gun back in Robbie's hand, which my brother had trained on him under the streetlight, not letting on that it was empty. I stood looking at Luke. But he wouldn't even look at me now.

The Richmonds broke away first and were halfway up the Stone Steps by the time we caught up. Daniel tossed down a flowerpot, which shattered on the ledge near my head, throwing dirt all over me. Robbie shot up at him. Name-calling started. We called them sissies. We called them fags. We called them sissy-fags. They were not exactly speechless. But for all they yelled back—hicks, racists, John Brown killers—it was a lame sputter of dirty words. Then they darted off down the alley like the wusses they were, leaving my heart to pound like three or four hearts, my father's in me the biggest and angriest of them.

Seconds later, we heard strange shouting above. Older, deeper voices. When we got to the top of the steps, two shadows were stretched like giants around the three smaller shadows that were the Richmonds. By the streetlight at the far end of the alley, we could make out only slivers of faces and arms. But we knew who they had to be: Ricky and his buddy, as angry as they could be.

And they thought the Richmonds had thrown the stones at them!

Daniel broke for the stone wall, and Alex ran between a parked car and the Harper House. That left Luke trapped between the two hulking shadows closing in. His skinny shadow darted this way, then that, but they had him. One of the big silhouettes latched hold of him and started shaking him. We could hear Luke's choked-off shouts.

With Daniel scampering over the rock wall and Alex hightailing it out of the alley, suddenly, the Richmonds' porch light came on, and out came Mr. Richmond, kitchen knife raised over his head.

"What's going on out here!" he roared in his best John Brown voice.

The shadowy man dropped Luke's limp body like a sack. When Mr. Richmond yelled out that he was calling the police, both silhouettes started slinking back in our direction, their shadows thinning into wiggly rubber bands on the side of the Harper House. As they came near, my brothers and I crouched down. The streetlight by the church caught their faces, whitened them like eggs—Ricky Hardaway and Snake Wilson! They disappeared down the Stone Steps.

Mr. Richmond, crunching hard across the moon-white gravel, ran to where Luke was sitting up, holding his shoulder. Daniel backed down the rock wall like a spider, and together they bent down over Luke. Mr. Richmond then shouted to Alex, who was standing under the streetlight at the far end of the alley, to call the police. He ran off, and when the front door of the Richmond place slammed shut, the alley went quiet.

For long, quiet minutes, Mr. Richmond and Daniel stayed crouched down beside Luke's sitting form. My brothers and I, hiding on the knoll at the other end of the alley, were hugging the dark cover of the slope—wide-eyed, hearts pounding, as knotted up inside as the tree roots we clung to. What in the hell had we done?

CHAPTER XIX: SIRENS IN THE NIGHT

OON, BLUE LIGHTS WHIPPED through the dark trees on the hill, and a ranger Jeep roared into the alley, its headlights flooding down the walls of the Harper House, catching our sweaty faces. A ranger stepped through the blaze of headlights to where Mr. Richmond and Daniel were kneeling over Luke. Over the racing engine of the Jeep, we could hear the crackle of a walkie-talkie. Robbie whispered that Luke really looked hurt. We waited, the thumps of our hearts like cantaloupes trying to burst open.

Finally Luke stirred, sat up, but had trouble standing.

"Broken ribs probably," Jerry whispered.

He had news for us. No one would blame Ricky Hardaway or his buddy when they found the busted picture window and learned what we did to start it all.

As if in answer, a siren cut through the night. We ducked down. It seemed to come from every direction—up the rock wall, over the glass slope, screaming down the sides of the church. As we looked helplessly at each other, I realized just how desperate our situation was.

More sirens came wailing down into town. Through the trees we could see Sergeant Kelly's police car flashing. Behind it was the Friendship Fire Company ambulance, its bubble light zipping around. Behind that came a state police car, low, wide, and sparkling brown under the streetlight, with antennas all over, arching from trunk to hood, a huge yellow star on the door. If only this could be a bad dream.

Up the back hill, the three of us ran like crazy. Limbs whipped at us like neighbors angry at our escape. At Church Street, Jerry took off first for Jefferson's Rock, Robbie next, then me, the three of us running helter-skelter through helicopter blades of red and blue flashes from the lower street.

We met up in the woods past the old Civil War hospital and headed for the shadow of Jefferson's Rock beyond. As the sirens became more and more distant, we could hear our own heavy breathing, the weeds and branches breaking around us, the river rushing below, and the whine of cars over on the highway. When we cleared the tree line, we used the gravestones in Robert Harper Cemetery to pull our tired legs up the hill. Everywhere were large shadows looming close.

We were too scared, breathless, and desperate to escape to blame each other, but in the moonlight, I caught my brothers glancing at me. Robbie looked at me as if I had burned down the church and thrown myself off the cliffs, I had ruined my life so much. For once I was miles crazier than they were—I had started it all by shooting out the big window, then terrorizing Luke with the BB gun. If I didn't know better, I'd say they were scared of me.

We sneaked across Philmore, our shadows as tall as telephone poles, and at the town park melted back into the darkness. I could hear Robbie whimpering, he was so frightened. With Jerry in the lead, we ran one, two, three down High Street, our sneakers clapping down and popping out echoes. Dog after dog rose up and barked at us from the porches. When we heard another siren coming down the hill, we charged into old man Boatwright's weedy backyard and crouched down. Another fire truck passed, swinging its slow red flashes through the night, painting up our faces like Indians. When the Boatwrights' back porch light came on, we made for the woods at the far edge of the weedy yard, disappeared in them, and followed the big rocks of the dried-up creek bed down to River Road.

Once on the coal-covered road, we were in a kind of sooty blackness, except for a tiny star of light bursting down the tracks from the railroad station. It was enough to see sweat on our faces. Every cop in the county would be looking for us, Jerry said in a hushed voice. There would be no going back to town, not now, not ever.

He turned and started up River Road. Robbie and I followed, stepping in ruts until we reached the crossing, where light from the station rode the rails to us in silver lines. Jerry was there waiting for us, standing in the middle of the tracks, his silhouette as rigid as the crossing signal. For the first time, the three of us were brothers, guilty as hell and in it together.

We headed up the tracks in the night, the moon overhead drifting under clouds and only a few stars to see by.

Jerry had a book of matches with only a few left and didn't want to use any of them unless he absolutely had to. No one spoke. No one said where we were going, either. In our hearts we knew where we were going—to the empty white house up the river. It was leading us to it like letters on a Ouija board. All our memories started there. We were running home.

CHAPTER XX: RETURN TO THE WHITE HOUSE

A S MUCH AS WE TRIED to be quiet, we clinked gravel against the rails and ended up using the rails themselves as a guide, tapping our toes against them every few steps like blind men using walking sticks. When the moon drifted behind clouds, it was too dark to see even the outline of the cliffs above John Brown's Cave. Suddenly, with his arm outstretched like a school crossing signal, Jerry stopped, stopping us, too.

"Shh! Somebody's back there," he whispered.

We turned and stared and waited, the black night filling our eyes.

"Nobody's back there," Robbie said.

"No, I heard somebody."

We inched on, silent for the longest time. Then Jerry whispered that they would be looking for us and Ricky Hardaway together. Mr. Richmond would get the rangers after us for sure, Robbie added. Not that that was our biggest concern. *Teen correctional facility.* Dad had threatened us with it enough times. Then my brothers fell silent.

I knew what they were thinking. Robbie was the first to bring it up.

"Man, Josh, why'd you shoot Luke like that?"

"The gun was empty, stupid!" I shot back.

"Yeah, but he didn't know that."

"'Cause he thinks he's better than us," I said.

I couldn't hide my jealousy of Luke for being who he was, when I had to be who I was.

The horrible thing was, I didn't hate anyone tonight except my father. I had gone to confession today. Now I had every bad thought and feeling in the world, thanks to him. Cowmint was no longer something special. Shakespeare was just a dead guy who once wrote funny words. And every mirror I looked into now showed me and my brothers all the same. I stood up on the rails, the whole world behind me burning for good.

At the underpass, we found the lane to the old Catholic school property. But with only a few lights across the river to see by, we wandered off the lane and ended up in briar patches. Robbie, in getting himself unstuck, almost stepped down into the river. Eventually Jerry got us to the chapel ruins, where Robbie then walked right into the armless statue of the Virgin Mary and cried out when he felt the granite face in front of his eyes.

"Shh!" Jerry said.

"I heard it, too," I said.

Behind us, a twig snapped. Then another. Someone was definitely following us.

We crouched down and waited, waited for so long that

we couldn't tell one minute from ten. At last, Jerry whispered that it could have been a deer. We moved on and finally broke through the dark woods. Grandma's house, looming on the knoll beyond, was ghostly white in the moonlight.

My brothers and I could never get ready enough for it. When we were younger and rode out this lane to see Grandma, every time we came upon the white house, it took our breath away. Even tonight, we were filled with the same old questions. *Why was it back here? How could it stay spotless white for so long? Why did it look twice as high as it should be?* So many windows, too, all black and curtainless and so close together you could reach out of one into another.

"It's like a giant gravestone in our family," Jerry said tonight.

That, I thought, was a cool comment, even now.

"Or a big refrigerator," said Robbie.

He would say this.

As we walked toward the house across the frosty moonlit meadow, we kept glancing back at the dark edge of the woods, waiting for the shape of the person to come through, following us.

"Probably the bum," Robbie said. "Or the cops."

"Way back on the railroad tracks, too?" Jerry said.

I tried not to be scared as long as I had my brothers on either side of me. When we reached the house, Jerry stopped and looked up at the zillion windows—even he was scared now. Being here in the daytime was one thing. At night was another.

He opened the front door, and we stepped into complete

blackness. The air was moldy-smelling and the floor gritty, making our sneakers noisy. Jerry told us to be quiet—the bum, if he was here, might be upstairs.

We started feeling our way down the hall, bumping into each other like dominoes. Jerry got a face full of cobweb, Robbie hooked his finger on a nail in the wall, and I was stepping on both their heels.

Once on the stairs, we had the handrails to hold onto. Step after creaky step we went up, with Jerry in the lead, the darkness over us like a low ceiling we were always about to bump our heads into. As we turned and followed the banister down the hall, I remembered a story from catechism years ago about a boy trapped inside a whale. The boy prayed and prayed in the dark stomach of the whale, until it spit him out, and when he came out, he was happy because God had forgiven him. I hoped God would forgive us tonight, too.

When we passed the room in this identical house that was where Luke's room was in the Richmonds' house, I whispered: "What if he dies?"

"He won't die," Jerry said back. "He was sitting up."

Then he stopped. He heard something, he said. He struck one of the matches, and it sparked, and a dotlike flame grew until light flickered around the cruddy brown stomach of the whale we were inside. He held the match out as far as he could—at night, it was the ugliest, barest house that could ever be. Down the hall were many dark doors, like a prison.

The match soon burned out, and again the belly of the

whale was pitch dark around us. Up more stairs we went, following a handrail that felt dustier the farther along we went. Things were crunching underfoot. I imagined everything from bird bones to Mom's green elbow macaronis.

"Shh! Smell that?" Robbie said.

"That's from the match, stupid," Jerry said.

The higher we went, the more light from stars came into the house. Soon we could make out walls and doorways. As we passed empty room after empty room, I started saying what was in the same room in the Richmonds' house. I was talking to try to scare away the dark that was scaring me.

"Here's Daniel's bedroom," I said. "Here's the fancy room with the sofa Mom likes. Here's Alex's room for practicing the clarinet in."

Jerry told me to be quiet.

When we came to Mr. Richmond's room, it was Jerry who said Mr. Richmond would hate us forever now. At the top of the house, he struck another match.

"Dad's room," he said.

We stood looking in at the grungy mattress on the floor. Nothing was around it—no food wrappers or cigarette butts. Just a lonely little stained mattress at the top of the house. It was the first time since the house had been abandoned by the church years ago that the three of us were here together at the same time.

I took a step farther in than my brothers and stood at the window, looking for cop car lights on the lane, then downriver, seeing only the faintest glow of house lights from town. I wondered if one was Mr. Richmond's house, or even Luke's room, where he might be lying injured. In that instant, I felt the houses were talking to each other, like lighthouse beacons winking at each other.

"You ever come out here, Robbie?" Jerry asked.

"Sometimes."

"You, Josh?"

"Sometimes."

"Me, too."

For the first time, we weren't all lying about it.

We stepped back out into the hall. Suddenly, there was the clink of a cigarette lighter. A flame burst up, lighting up the old hallway around us—and there stood Robbie with a smug grin, holding Dad's good cigarette lighter. It had a Confederate flag on it and the words, "Forget, hell!" With the flame burning under his face, my brother looked like a pie-faced Frankenstein. Jerry was furious that he had had the lighter all this time. They fought over it, the flame wavering around. Jerry won, and now we practically had a torch to lead us out of here.

We went back downstairs, peering into room after room, with the flame from the lighter, on full force, licking up the blackness. On the floor was a strange grit, and on the walls thick dust. The house had aged over the summer and seemed so different from how it had looked in the daytime, with sunlight coming in.

Soon the lighter got too hot to keep lit, and we were back to stumbling through the dark. Light from the stars, coming in windows on one side of the house, helped. On the third floor, we came to the big door at the end of hall. Jerry put his hand on the knob.

"Don't!" Robbie hissed.

Our brother turned halfway around. "Why not? She's dead!"

Grandma was dead, but that didn't mean her ghost wasn't still around. Jerry turned the knob, the door creaked open, and the flame of Dad's cigarette lighter, back on for an instant, showed a room as big as John Brown's Cave. We stepped in. Like the other rooms, this one was empty, except for a mousetrap in the corner, which was empty, too. The church had left nothing when it cleared out, not even a chair for the bum. With the lighter getting hot again, soon we were back in blackness.

"Old bitch," Jerry said, stepping farther in.

"Shh," said Robbie.

"What? She gonna get me from the grave?" Jerry stomped down on the floor just to show his contempt. "Old bitch! Old bitch! *She's* the reason Dad's the way he is."

Suddenly, there was a blast of light from behind. It was so sudden and bright we were more blinded than scared. But even with white spots in our eyes, we knew instantly the big, solid figure standing there.

Dad!

This was the end. I felt my insides drop like the five floors in this house.

He put his hand over the beam, choking off all but a

few rays of light, his fingertips glowing red. The light that escaped lit up the underside of his face, making creepy, deep shadows.

"Shh!" he said, the hiss of his voice sounding like a giant egg slicer over the darkness.

He came toward us and, in a strange, low voice, asked what we were doing here. Jerry crumbled like old Sheetrock, and Robbie probably peed himself. Both started blaming each other.

"Never mind now," he said, stepping past us.

With one hand cupped over the flashlight, he eased the door shut with the other. Then he stepped back and switched off the light, dropping us into darkness.

"We're not the only ones here," he said.

CHAPTER XXI: SECRETS IN THE STAIRS

I COULD HEAR ROBBIE'S HEARTBEAT JUMP up over mine.

"Who?" Jerry whispered. "The bum?"

"Bum, hell," our father growled. "Who do you think?"

Ricky Hardaway!

"He should be downstairs by now. Just stand still," he ordered.

We grew into hickory trees, we were so knotted up. In the long, hard minutes that passed, Dad went after us in the dark, his voice a snarling whisper.

"I wanna know who in the hell was the ringleader in smashing that John Brown picture window tonight!"

In the pitch black of the room, I could feel the heat of his glare, smell his pipe smoker's breath.

"Answer me. Who beat up those Richmond boys? Who threw rocks at Ricky?"

I waited for Jerry or Robbie to crack. The silence was awful. Dad, meanwhile, was breathing down our necks.

"Come on, dammit, the rangers told me everything anyway. You're all in big trouble. Let's hear it."

But as more and more seconds passed and none of us broke, our father's angry voice settled into a growling, cursing mutter. He told us that, earlier tonight, before we caused all the commotion in town, the state police, out of sheer coincidence, had gone to Ricky's shack on Hog Alley.

"Apparently, they had an arrest warrant for him."

"Arrest warrant?" Jerry hissed.

"Yes, arrest warrant. For selling drugs."

"So they're after Ricky?" Robbie asked brightly.

"And you all, too, now!" Dad snapped back.

The rest of the story was that when our father came home and found half the town in the street, thanks to our mayhem, he went out looking for us and spotted Ricky's old Chevy stalled this side of the railroad crossing and figured where he was heading. Somehow in the dark he must have passed him on River Road, or in the woods along the lane.

"But you all were impossible to miss," he muttered. "You sounded like a damn herd of buffalo wearing bells!"

He took a step away, his shoes crunching something on the floor.

"I should turn you all over to Ricky," he added in an angry whisper. "Teach you all a lesson. Your poor mother is worried sick—and, Jerry, don't think I didn't hear what you just said about your grandmother."

Then he was silent for a moment. Grandma's ghost, meanwhile, was yelling at us, and at our father, too, for sparing the rod. Finally, I broke my silence.

"Is Luke . . . ?"

"It's not good," he answered back. "Neither is that damn John Brown figure. You all have got some explaining to do."

He switched the flashlight back on, again letting only the fewest shafts of light out, and started looking around at the old walls of his mother's bedroom, the way he would in our attic when he had a mind to check for cracks in the plaster. A dead mud wasps' nest was scattered on the floor like dirt. He stopped to say he was surprised there weren't crows or raccoons in here by now.

As worried as I was about Luke, it was fascinating to see my father in this house for the first time since I was really young. Somehow the house got smaller around him. Or he got bigger.

"Well, I can't wait here all night," he said, not bothering to whisper anymore. "Come on. Maybe I can get you all back to town before they arrest you for—" He had started toward the door, only to stop and turn to us, a perplexed look on his face. "Or maybe we should stay the hell put? Till I figure out what's going on?"

A moment later, he took his hand off the top of the flashlight, and the beam shot loose. Grandma's room was as brown as the inside of our lunch bags. He opened the door and stepped out into the dark house, shining the light through the musty air along the walls, down the steps, and between the floors. I kept my eyes on the beam, which shined on and on, as if lost in a black hole. The darkness around me was less scary that way.

"Ricky!"

Dad's voice ran up and down our bones and the bones of the house at the same time, from the dark banisters to the shadowy doorways.

"If you're out here, boy, you better say!"

But the big house answered back with emptiness and silence.

"Maybe he left," Robbie whispered.

"Maybe, hell."

"Ricky!" Robbie called out over the banister, his voice echoing down.

Letting my brother yell down into the dark cavern of the house, scaring the blackness out with his big mouth, Dad started down the hall, but soon stopped at a black window to peer out into the night, no doubt to see if there were any cop car lights on the lane. The fact that he moved on slowly said there weren't any. He almost seemed to be taking his time.

A few steps later, with Jerry and me right behind him, Dad stopped to peek into a room, causing us to bump into him. The room, he remembered aloud, had been crammed full of pew ends and lecterns when he was a boy.

"We had hand-carved ivory angels stored in there, too," he said, suddenly going off into memories. "Finest you'd ever see. Bet they were a hundred years old, some of them. Worth something, too, because someone sure as hell took off with them."

Robbie, catching up, had Dad's good lighter flicked on and was looking around at the dirty walls and baseboards, trying to act like our father, as if he knew how to inspect the house like an expert. Dad, shining his flashlight off in another direction, found a shiny beer can on a windowsill.

"That dumb SOB Ricky. He'll end up just like his father," he grumbled, roaming the beam around the walls and floor.

"How's he related to us anyway?" Jerry asked, trying to sound sour about asking, though it was all part of his brownnosing number on Dad.

Still, it was a question that in our family seemed to take three hundred years to ask.

Dad shined the flashlight in Jerry's white face. "You telling me you don't know?"

My brother shook his head, and Dad went back to roaming the beam around the walls and floor.

"He's your Uncle Earl's oldest boy." He turned to Jerry again. "You mean, your damn mother never told you all?"

"Uncle Earl?" said Jerry.

"Yes, Uncle Earl," Dad said, starting down to the fourth floor, his flashlight beam zipping here and there, checking every possible hiding place.

"He's not here, is he?" Robbie said, catching up, sounding disappointed.

Jerry, meanwhile, was still standing on the top step. I turned and looked back at him. I knew what he was thinking. Uncle Earl was the most embarrassing drunk in our family. No wonder Ricky turned out the way he did.

Down the long hallway we went. Dad was poking his head into empty room after empty room, going on about solid-cherry prayer desks and gold altar cups. In the strangest way, I thought he sounded happy, remembering how the house had been, like the way I felt over at the Richmonds' among their nice things. By the time we reached the second floor, he wasn't bothering to lower his voice or be cautious anymore.

"... half these damn rooms were filled to the ceiling with oak chapel chairs, brass candleholders, what have you. Stained-glass windows, old vestments—hell, we even had a Cardigan font full of jewels. You'd have thought the damn Vatican was right up the road."

"Wow, this place was cooler than Mr. Richmond's," Robbie let out.

"Well, I hope to tell you," Dad said back. "Wait a minute now." He swung the flashlight around like a searchlight, across the dark rectangles of doorways that stood in a row like thick, square devils watching us. "We had a solid brass Vatican weathervane around here somewhere. Somebody stole that, too."

"Uncle Earl probably stole it," Jerry muttered.

Dad spun around.

"Jerry, you're so all-fired to say something bad about your Uncle Earl, aren't you? Know something good for a change. He was a deacon in the church."

Jerry stood speechless. Robbie and I did, too.

"A deacon?" our brother finally said.

"At one time, yes, he was a damn deacon," Dad said.

Our father looked down at the floor, before scuffing it with his shoe.

"Hell, I even thought of being priest myself at one time," he said.

I didn't know whether my brothers believed him, but I did, though I wasn't sure why. We were just inside the kitchen, and our father was stabbing the beam through the dusty darkness to a spot in the middle of the floor.

"Your Uncle Earl sat right there every Sunday night, reading your grandmother the Psalms."

My brothers and I remembered the spot as where he and Grandma sat and argued at the table about everything from the problem with the pump house to the problem with the White House.

"Dad."

My voice was like a brick wall waiting for my father to crash into it. I could have never guessed what I would ask next.

"Who's that priest in the picture at home? The one you hid from us?"

Dad walked in a circle through the dark kitchen, shining the light on the floor.

"None of your business. That's who," he said.

He stopped, turned, and stood with his back to us. Seconds passed. The house was quiet around us. Jerry wheeled around, crunching something under his shoe.

"Dad, who?" my brother demanded.

Another second passed, and still our father was quiet. Then he came toward us, flashlight beam raked across his chest and face like a spotlight. At the last second, he turned and shined the light in a tight beam on the wall. He was like a car with no driver, its headlights aimed off the road and into the woods at nothing.

"How many years the damn archdiocese blamed *me* for everything stole out of this house," he muttered. "Did you know that? Said *I* should have kept an eye on this place."

He spun around, the beam whipping across the walls.

"*Me?* As if I had nothing better to do. Hell, I was trying to raise you all. I couldn't come out here every day!"

"Dad!"

"Jerry, stop shouting, damn your heart!"

The house snapped silent, and the four of us stood quiet, the flashlight casting monsterlike shadows of us.

"Okay, bigmouths," our father finally said. "You all wanna know *who* so damn bad. You'll find out on your own anyhow, knowing you."

Flashlight in hand, our father pivoted, the beam cutting the black air like a lightsaber. At the same time, my brothers and I turned and faced him, lining up in the dark like cadets. Dad stood looking at each of us.

"There was a certain priest out here at one time," he said. "All the kids loved him. Could throw a damn football seventy yards, on the run, too."

He paused as if we should try guessing. In the scattered glow of the flashlight, I could see his profile frowning.

"Father O'Cleary," he finally said, switching the flashlight off.

The house, plunging into darkness, stood pitch-black around us. Echoing in my mind was this name *Father O'Cleary*. Who was he? I had never heard of him before.

I stood thinking furiously. Jerry and Robbie stood silently beside me, surely doing the same. A second later, Dad's voice broke through the darkness.

"But the man wasn't what people thought."

I could hear him take a step away.

"Not by a damn sight," he said, his voice bearing down.

My voice finally eked out. "Why?"

My brothers and I, wrapped in blackness, stood waiting for the answer. The whole blackened house stood waiting. Would we finally find out what was *following* our father?

CHAPTER XXII: CONFESSION IN THE DARK

CAUSE HE WAS A DAMN thief," Dad said, switching the flashlight back on, his voice quivering as the beam of light glazed his face. "Stole church funds. Thousands and thousands and *thousands* of dollars. And probably whatever else he could. There. Now you know."

He turned and took a step away, his shoes crunching bird poop on the floor, but not before I saw deep lines in his face, grooves filled with sadness.

"... cooking the books, and I suspected him," he said, shining the flashlight into the musty veil of darkness over the house. "Suspected him, but ..."

Then, I couldn't believe it—he laughed. But it was a short bitter laugh.

"You know, I actually admired the damn man. All of us did." He turned to us, but didn't say anything for a long minute. "*Admired him?* Can you believe that?"

He stood looking at us, but also looking right through us, the points of light in his eyes like penlights.

"Enough, dammit, to wanna join the priesthood."

All of a sudden, he burst out in a wheezy pipe smoker's laugh.

"Even called me," he said, slapping his leg as he turned to us, his face filled with a scary smile, toothy and wild in the bouncing light, "the son he never had."

I watched the curled ends of his chilling smile fall, wilting down like tears ready to drop.

"Then, the man tried to buy my silence—tried to *buy* it! A Catholic priest, in line for archbishop, mind you."

I stood terrified of all that was hurting my father, of all that I didn't understand but was smoldering around in the dark behind him. Jerry and Robbie, meanwhile, were frozen beside me, poured into the floor like concrete.

"You boys know how much ten thousand dollars was to a small retreat like this one?" he asked.

I waited for Jerry to answer. Or Robbie. I had never heard my father talk about money this way before. Finally, Jerry's voice peeked out of the inky darkness.

"Why, Dad?" he said. "Why didn't you . . . ?"

Dad, starting to turn away, whirled back around.

"Tell somebody?" He thumped his chest with his fist, the flashlight beam shaking around. "I did tell somebody!"

His voice clapped up the insides of the house. Taking a deep breath, he stood up straight, his shadow rising up the wall.

"Now listen, the three of you, 'cause I don't want to have to repeat this. *Josh*, you especially."

I felt my spine tingle at the mention of my name. Dad

stood with his back to us for a moment, his shadow climbing, trying to get away from him.

"I *confided*, you might say, in another priest they had out here. A 'stand-in,' they called him."

He took a step away, his shoes crunching more bird poop.

"But what I said in confidence . . . it got out. And a few busybodies around here started asking questions. Twistin' things around."

Dad spun around, his face in flames.

"Took my confession—a sacred Catholic confession made right down there in that chapel, on this very lane," he said, stabbing his finger into the shadows of the house, "and divulged it. *Divulged* it!"

He whirled around as if he'd like to grab and throw something, like a lamp or a vase, but the house was empty, from corner to corner, top to bottom.

"I should have sued or something! Divulging a damn confession, then falsely accusing me? I should have—should have—"

He stood sputtering until he just stomped his shoe down on the floor, and the house grunted, as if punched in the gut.

"Before I knew it, it was too damn late. This place was shut down. Penniless. Your poor grandparents fired—hell, evicted!"

"*Evicted?*"

Jerry's scared voice scampered up the skinny railings of the house.

"Yes, fired and evicted." Dad took another step off, but turned and came right back. "Unofficially anyway." He pointed his finger at us. "Now don't go repeating it. Not to anybody, you hear?"

Jerry pushed past me.

"But you said they retired, Dad."

Our father popped out a bizarre laugh that sounded as if he was laughing and crying at the same time.

"Yes, I know I did," he said. "They were 'retired' all right. Blamed, evicted, and retired. Hell, the church even pointed fingers at your Uncle Earl—he was the one who kept the books for O'Cleary." He looked off into the darkness. "All because I *did* speak up."

With the flashlight beam shooting up the folds of his shirt, our father's face was shadowed from the top down, making him look like a zombie.

"Even tried to say I should have spoken up sooner—" He broke out laughing again, laughing as if dying. Then he turned to us. "But I didn't want to bring scandal to the church. This was my home."

My brothers and I watched as he peered up, as if ghosts in the stairs were suddenly calling to him, *"Psst! Psst!"*

"Maybe I could have . . ." His voice faded as he gazed farther up into the shadowy cavern of the house that rose over him like a starless heaven. ". . . saved this damn place."

His lips, as he spoke, barely moved.

"Saved myself, too. Years and years of grief. My mother—" He dropped his head and turned away.

". . . she and Dad never knew. Never knew my 'confession' ruined them. Hell, I never even told your all's poor mother."

Then he pivoted and looked squarely at me.

"Josh, maybe now you'll see why I was so damn upset you went over to that church today and took confession from that man?"

I nodded. I nodded as hard as I could. But I knew my father couldn't see me in the darkness. I was like a crocodile hiding under black water.

"That 'Father Ron' character—" The flashlight beam dropped to the floor. I could feel my father struggling—struggling to just stand up in this house, struggling to talk. "You know, he just reminds me of O'Cleary," he said, in a laugh that would have been better off a cry. "Same damn tricky smile."

Again he drifted away from us, and again the flashlight went off. The big house stood black and quiet for a long moment. You could hear creaks in every one of her twenty rooms, as if she were a big ship filled with water and about to explode.

"But know this," he said, his firm voice returning. "I've been trying to protect you damn boys from another O'Cleary."

I was floating in outer space, there was so much darkness around me, as if all the light in the world was gone except for the sharp white burn of my father's words. Dad wanting to be a priest? His confession twisted against him? Grandma and Granddad evicted? No wonder he hated the church. Dad was hung out to dry by the people he trusted.

They snitched on him. He didn't do anything wrong. He was screwed.

As I stood here in my grandmother's house, my mind blown away by what our father had just revealed to us, the only thing that kept my feet on the ground was the feeling that I was actually impressed that he had admitted this to us, in this house, of all places.

I now knew in my heart why my father was so angry all the time. For that matter, I knew why Uncle Earl was left to drink himself to death in the doorways around Charles Town, when he had once been a deacon in the church and when he had sat at the kitchen table with Grandma Connors every Sunday evening for twenty years, reading the Psalms.

"Now listen," our father said, standing up straight again, his stern voice back as if the moment never happened, "we can't stand around here talkin' all night. You three are gonna have to go up to the police station when we get back. So you better get your stories straight right now."

In the dim light, I caught sight of Jerry. Robbie was peering in, too. We each knew what the other was thinking. It was better to know something even this sad about our father, rather than just hate him.

CAREFULLY, DAD OPENED the door to the back porch, which also led down to the cellar, where there was another door to the outside. We made our way down rickety steps. At the bottom, Dad stood shining the light around at a barren concrete floor that for some reason smelled of mulch.

"Dad, what's Sergeant Kelly going to do?" Jerry asked.

"I don't know. I really don't."

"No, I mean to Ricky."

Dad's head flicked up.

"Ricky? Well, they sent him away for a year the last time. This time it'll probably be ten."

"Ten?" Robbie and I both said. "Ten years?"

"They won't be lenient, no."

"But Uncle Earl'll be dead in ten years."

"Probably so, Jerry."

"Grandma would do something," Robbie put in.

Dad had a definite response to that—"The shit she would. Your damn grandmother would turn that crazy Ricky Hardaway in the first chance she got, then ask for a reward. And don't stand there and tell me what Mr. Richmond would do either—I don't understand you kids. An hour ago you were hitting that boy with stones!"

"You said he stole the chapel bell!" Jerry said.

"I didn't say to stone him for it!"

Jerry took a step back.

I spoke up: "You keep saying we're not like the Richmonds! Then we must be like Ricky."

Dad shined the light on the floor. "That's not what I meant, and don't go getting too smart for your britches— and don't stand there smiling either. It's not funny."

But it was funny. An hour ago we were hitting Ricky Hardaway with stones, not to mention shooting at the Richmonds with an empty BB gun, which Dad hadn't brought up yet, and now it was gnawing at us that Ricky had a drunk for a father, a drunk who also had once been a deacon. It seemed it didn't matter how close you were to God, you could still end up rock-bottom.

"I suppose," Dad said, dropping the beam on the floor in front of him, "the Christian thing to do would be for somebody to help Ricky."

Jerry's voice rose up like a tent. "But you said he left."

"Shit, no, he hasn't left."

My brothers and I turned and looked at each other, our faces lit in slivers.

"My guess is he's right out there in the barn," Dad said. "Or somewhere nearby, hiding."

Jerry dashed to the window first, then Robbie and me, but all we could see was the glare on the glass from Dad's flashlight.

"How do you know, Dad?" Jerry said.

"How do I know? 'Cause this damn house is the only place he has to go."

We thought this old house was the only place *we* had left to go.

But before any of us could answer, Robbie's voice hissed out in the darkness.

"Lights, Dad!"

CHAPTER XXIII: LIGHTS ON THE LANE

OBBING THROUGH THE DARK field along the river were half a dozen flashlights!

"Shit, the police!" Dad said. "I bet they found that damn boy's car. Come on. If I get you boys back to town, maybe I can talk 'em into not dragging you all off in squad cars in the middle of the night. Out here they will, sure as hell!"

Telling Robbie to grab the lantern, he took off for the stairs. Halfway up, he stopped and put up his hand, causing us to collide into him.

"Listen!"

We stood there in the dark. At first we didn't hear anything. Then, through the old walls of the house came a sound—the slow ringing of a bell!

Dong. Dong. Dong.

Dad shot forward, leaving us to catch up. Trampling on each other's heels, we ran after him. Outside, in the dark night, the bell was striking loud and clear, coming from behind the house, in the direction of the garage. Dad's flashlight beam, meanwhile, was bouncing over the dark weeds as he ran.

By the time we caught up, the bell had stopped ringing, and Dad, standing in the waist-deep weeds in front of the garage, had his light trained on Ricky Hardaway's face! Washed out, it looked like a mask.

"Look, Bill," Ricky was saying and pointing, "I found it! I found it!"

Dad stabbed the light into the wooden shell of the building—on the floor, gray and dusty-looking, sat the chapel bell! It looked like the embattled helmet of a giant.

Jerry ran up and put his hands all over it. Dad put the light on Ricky's grinning face again, held it there, but said nothing.

"I found it," Ricky said again, as if nothing else bad was happening and it was normal to hide on our grandmother's old land in the middle of the night and find a stolen bell while he was there.

"Found it, my foot. Ricky," Dad said, "the whole damn sheriff's department's heading up the lane. They'll find you back here as sure as hell. Me, too, for that matter."

Dad lowered the light on Ricky's scratched-up hands and thistle-covered blue jeans. Then, with a sweep of the light around the garage behind him, he asked if anyone else was hiding back here.

"Where in the hell's that other boy you were with tonight?" Dad asked.

Ricky swore he was alone.

"Well, come on then," Dad said.

He was practically towing Ricky out from behind the old garage door with the beam.

"Everybody get going," Dad said, starting off in the lead.

Then he stopped, pointed the white beam at the bell, and told us to find a tarp or something to throw over it. We did more than that. My brothers and I piled old bumpers and paint cans around it, then threw burlap sacks and bits of hay all over the gold top of it. The sheriff's department would have to call a backhoe if they wanted to uncover it.

Then Dad headed off toward the barn, leaving us in the dark with Ricky, whose white T-shirt was practically glowing.

"Hey, cous," he said, a goofy smile in his voice.

The guilt was piling up inside me. So was curiosity. But all at once, I figured it out. Mom was right. Ricky hadn't been stealing a bell in the middle of the night on that river. He had been bringing it back!

Dad swung the light around to make sure we were following, and soon Ricky's legs were long and shadowy in the light cast on the ground ahead. When we caught up, he was saying to our father that he didn't hit that Richmond kid, that Snake Wilson did. Jerry spoke up. It would be like Snake to hit a kid, he told Dad. Snake hit bumpers and axles all day long with a sledgehammer in his father's junkyard.

"Ricky," Dad said, his flashlight hacking up the darkness, flashing across trees, darting off into the night, then back again to blaze on the ground, "you don't have to convince me."

That, I thought, was more than fair of him.

With Dad in the lead, we circled around through the high weeds, then on toward the pear trees along the river. Soon, big, hard pears lay everywhere. Robbie whispered it was like walking on duckpin bowling balls. Dad, his flashlight beam bouncing, told us not to leave tracks in the mud. I came to a stop.

"Look!" I hissed.

They were all under Dad's flashlight beam, a hundred of them, no, a thousand, growing as far as the eye could see, the same fuzzy pointed leaves and purple flowers and square stems and greenest berries—a whole field of cowmint!

Dad flooded the ground with light.

"I'll be damned," he said, his voice whispering off into the night.

Robbie, with a low whistle, squatted down and ran his hands over the tops of them. There must be a million, he said.

"We'll be rich!" Jerry sang out, acting all stupid.

"Shh!" said Robbie, glancing around.

Dad gave Jerry a frown. "Rich, my ass."

As he stooped down and put the flashlight beam up to a fuzzy leaf, I stepped as close to him as I dared. He looked at me for a full second, but said nothing. As he went on feeling the leaves and looking around at the cowmint ocean surrounding us, he asked himself in a whisper why in the world this plant would be growing way out here.

"I know why," I said.

He looked up at me. "Why?"

"God's growing them."

It was the only answer that made sense. They grew in the lot beside our house, which was beside a church, and they were growing here, on land which was once owned by the church. Since every plant book said there was no such plant, that left God.

My little comment, I was surprised to find, went unchallenged.

Leaning over with my father, inspecting the plants, I felt a tap on my back and turned to see, through the scattered flashlight beam, Ricky smiling down at me.

"Hey, bud, you found them miracle plants after all, didn't ya?" he said.

Jerry, meanwhile, in his own way, agreed it was divine providence, which gave our father no reason to frown at him, even as my brother started yanking up handfuls of the plant and stuffing the leaves into his pockets, saying he was getting rich now. Robbie did, too. All the while, lights in front of the house were bobbing closer.

At the last minute, Dad, saying he'd have to come back in the daytime for a closer look, switched off the flashlight, and we hurried off. We made our way by starlight down the riverbank, circling back past the white house and on toward the chapel ruins. It was slow going through the driftwood, and my foot snapped every dry branch it could find. My brothers whispered for me to be quiet, until Jerry finally kicked at me. Every now and then, the lantern Robbie was carrying clanked against his leg. The whole time, I could smell cowmint in the air.

Ahead, Dad was moving like a panther, with Ricky's T-shirt glowing behind him. Meanwhile, off to our right, the flashlights of cops in the field fluttered like fireflies toward the moon-white house. We were slipping away right under their noses!

Suddenly, light as bright as a train light burst through the trees, flooding the woods. Our old man's face looked pitted like a moon rock. He ducked down, yanking Ricky down, too. My brothers and I did the same. As a cop car bobbed up the lane, its headlights dancing through the woods, the five of us were crouched down like a band of Indians.

Dad hurried us on and soon had us crossing River Road in a crouched run, Ricky's white T-shirt streaking over the coal-blackened road. As we climbed the bank to the railroad tracks, ankle-deep gravel spilled down under us, sounding like a million noisy marbles rolling down. By the time we reached the top, I was sure we had woken up the whole county.

With gravel still rattling down below us, we stood on the solid cross-ties, looking upriver. A carnival of searchlights was now around the white house, the beams crisscrossing in the night. Robbie said it looked cool, but Dad was quick to tell him this was no game. Listen for trains, he whispered, as we started down the tracks—they could sneak up behind you like nothing on this earth.

As we walked, Dad didn't clink one stone against the rails, but the rest of us weren't so stealthy. Ricky definitely sounded like a damn buffalo wearing bells. The whole time, we were gaping into a night as pitch black as a coal bucket, with an eerie breeze that made the tracks feel as if we were inside a tunnel.

Suddenly, lights came up like nothing on this earth—a car on River Road! Before we could duck, headlights hit us from head to toe. Ricky's lanky silhouette was as tall as a totem pole for the world to see. In the panic, Dad had us down on our stomachs, hugging the rails. As the car passed, he turned and watched the taillights.

"Another damn cop car—Ricky, where's that other boy you were with tonight?" Dad asked again, his voice as angry as I had ever heard it.

"Him and me split up at the train station. Swear," said Ricky.

"You better hope so."

As we followed the long curve in the tracks around the cliffs under Lee Jackson's hotel, a red light appeared in the darkness ahead of us. It burned like an electric eye already aware of us. Dad's arm went up, stopping us. He was the first to figure it out. The back of a caboose—a train was stopped on the tracks!

CHAPTER XXIV: JOHN BROWN'S CAVE

THE ONLY PLACE LEFT TO go was up against the cliffs. Ricky must have scuffed half a pound of gravel getting his lanky legs over the rails, and Dad couldn't cuss enough to keep us quiet. By the light of the stars, I recognized the black outline of the cliffs. We were near the side entrance to John Brown's Cave, I said.

"Show me," Dad whispered, his pipe breath in my face.

Feeling my way into the weeds, I found the hard, bare ground of the pig path leading to the cave. Dad was right behind me, his hand cupped over the flashlight. Soon we all were tramping into the cave, Robbie at the rear, clanking the lantern.

Jerry wanted to hide far back in the cave, but Dad, still at the entrance, peering out, told him to stand still and be quiet for a moment. Where a train was stopped, he said, a brakeman was sure to be sniffing around.

Then, we all went farther back into the cave. We stepped through crevices, under overhangs, then through a kind of a dark doorway, where we reached a cavern. Dad was shining the flashlight around. Stalagmites and stalactites were everywhere—coming out of the floor, coming down from the ceiling, some glistening as if sweating, others just cruddy. Ricky started putting his hands out and touching all of them, as if walking through a hidden treasure. My brothers and I told Dad that the cave went back even farther and eventually came out up the tracks, but all he could say was, little good a damn cave would do us tonight.

Dad took the lantern from Robbie and shined the flashlight on it up close. It had a cracked globe, one mantle, and more rust in it than kerosene, but it might work. And work it did, flaring up on the first light, then nearly going out before settling to a low flame.

It was the first we saw of each other out of the darkness. Jerry and Robbie, sweaty-faced, stood gawking at Ricky, who was pale, his hands so black from grabbing the rails that he looked as if he had been crawling under a car.

Then Dad had to sit down, and the rock he sat on was in the middle of the floor like the cave's chandelier that had fallen. He reached into a pocket for his tobacco and started tapping his pipe against his palm, all the while gazing around the cave. In the low glow of the lantern, the jagged walls reached down toward him. The police, he said, would give up for the night soon enough, provided we hadn't given them a trail a blind man could follow. Then he looked back at Ricky, who had been silent.

"Ricky, you'll have to turn yourself in tonight," Dad said. "Or tomorrow at the latest—you hear me?"

"But I didn't hit that boy, Bill," Ricky whined back. "I like him."

"You *like* him?" Dad said, pipe clenched in his teeth. "Well, somebody sure didn't *like* him."

Ricky, getting nowhere with our father, sat on a rock and took out his pack of cigarettes. I waited for Dad to tell him this was no campout and not to smoke. Jerry stood aiming the flashlight around the cave. Robbie found his own rock to sit on, where he started flicking the cigarette lighter. It was a tiny torch, and the cave was big and shadowy. Everyone was quiet.

"Now, Jerry, Robbie, Josh, listen to me," Dad said in his sternest voice. "I wanna know something right here and now. Who in the hell busted out that damn window and started all this tonight?"

When he frowned mostly at Jerry, my brother went berserk in defense of himself, until he had no choice but to give me up.

"Josh," said my father, standing up, *"you shot that window out?"*

He stood gaping at me the same way he did when he opened the hub on my banana bike and found Johnson's Paste Wax inside instead of grease. Then he turned and stepped over to the corner of the cave and stood there for the longest time, his back to us, looking up, as if seeing John Brown's raid map scratched on the wall. Everybody got quiet. Twice he glanced back at me and said, "You? You shot out that window?"

"He thought the gun was empty, Dad," Jerry added.

That, I thought, was decent of my brother.

monds' house—now I understood the whole picture! The truth clapped out in a blinding white flash I had seen before. But this time, in my mind, both Grandma's house and the Richmonds' house became one, all their rooms, whether dark and lonely, filling and emptying, filling and emptying, up and around, down and around, backward and forward, fancy mirrors, chairs, and sofas—all appearing and disappearing, again and again. Then, like thunder and lightning, the moment was over.

In my astonishment, I found myself glancing around the cave. In my own way, I understood, too, why some rock icicles came down from the ceiling, while others came up from the floor. It was like the truth. That grew in two directions, too.

Dad pointed his finger around at us.

"Now don't you all go blabbing to your poor mother. She's been through enough."

My brothers and I sat quietly for a moment. I knew what they were thinking. So was I. Dad had known all this about Mr. Richmond, but never once used it against him to make himself seem better, as much as we had given him reason to. It was the kind of holding back we never expected from our father.

Outside, we could hear boxcars shifting and clanking. Jerry ran out toward the entrance. The train was moving, he called back. Lantern out, flashlight off, we made our way out of the cave and through the weeds.

CHAPTER XXVI: THE WALK HOME

WE TROOPED SILENTLY ALONG DOWN the tracks, looking down at the black ladder of rails and cross-ties, popping and pinging as they settled. In the pitch black, we could hear the slow freight rattling off in the distance. Dad had his hand cupped over the flashlight, letting out just a few rays. When we could no longer hear the train and the night seemed safe, Dad broke the silence.

"One more thing," he said. "Those boys don't have a mother around. Think about that."

What he meant was—think about our mother. Make her life easier.

When we reached the old power dam, we could hear a fire truck siren in the distance behind us. Or at least it sounded behind us. The cliffs played tricks with the sound. Dad craned his neck over the weedy bank of the raceway, but there were too many trees for him to see upriver.

On the long snake curve past the dam, the gravel between the rails was moon-white and thick. Jerry was walking fallen from the picture window where it had stood all my life. Glass had been swept up into a pile on the sidewalk.

"Old Josh murdered John Brown," Jerry muttered as we passed.

"Well, he kept looking at our house, asking for it," Robbie said.

"An accident was bound to happen," Dad said.

Our porch light was on, too, and there stood our poor mother, arms crossed in worry. Ricky waited down by the street while Dad, my brothers, and I plodded up the steps. Mom was relieved beyond words to see us.

"What in the hell do they all want, Katie?" Dad muttered, looking around the street.

"Well, I guess everybody's still worried about Luke."

The ambulance, she said, which left an hour ago, didn't take him, so he must not be badly hurt. Dad turned to my brothers and me and said we all had some apologizing to do, so we might as well start here and now.

"Bill?"

"Well, Katie, our family can't go on this way."

Dad wanted it all cleared up tonight. Mom stood there, arms folded a different way now. She tried to act annoyed that Dad had made a decision without her, but she was excited, even if a little scared, too.

Then, a big white sedan pulled up across the street, near the fallen figure of John Brown, and Lee Jackson got out and stood near its fancy hood ornament. Someone else was getting out on the passenger side.

Father Ron!

He stood in short sleeves and jeans.

Dad muttered something, then started down the steps. My brothers and I followed. Ricky, looking uneasy by himself on the street, was glad we were back. Dad, meanwhile, was taking his time crossing the street.

"Bill," said Lee Jackson, with a big phony smile, "we're glad to see everyone's okay."

Father Ron stepped around the front of the big car.

"Yes, we were worried about you all, Bill," he said.

"Worried about us?" Dad said back, finding himself standing face-to-face with a priest in blue jeans.

"Well, yes," said Lee Jackson. "Didn't you hear?"

"Hear what?"

"That house. Your mother's old place. It caught fire tonight."

Dad was so stiff his shadow moved more than he did.

"When?"

"Right now," said Father Ron.

"Just minutes ago," added Lee Jackson. "It's on the scanner."

Under the streetlight, I could see sweat on my father's face. He didn't know which way to go—left, right. Trying to see the flames upriver, he went up on his tiptoes and craned his neck all around. He even glanced at Lee Jackson's fancy car as if considering hopping in and racing off with it. He was practically zigzagging in the road when Sergeant Kelly's police cruiser came pulling up fast, idling high. Sergeant